Deadly Performance

I highly recommend **Deadly Performance** for its WWII London setting, well-paced plot, excellently written characters, and twisty mystery! 5 huge stars!

Christy's Cozy Corners

Secrets, historic detail, and a finely tuned mystery make **Deadly Performance** a delightfully captivating story in one of my favorite series!

Cozy Up With Kathy

Deadly Performance is an immersive, cozy mystery focusing on the history of the UK during WWII. It'll entertain the reader and bring them into another era of time that is so different than now.

Lori Van Buren, Novels Alive

Also from Kate Parker
The Deadly Series
Deadly Scandal
Deadly Wedding
Deadly Fashion
Deadly Deception
Deadly Travel
Deadly Darkness
Deadly Cypher
Deadly Broadcast
Deadly Rescue
Deadly Manor
Deadly Gamble
Deadly Performance
Deadly Village

The Victorian Bookshop Mysteries
The Vanishing Thief
The Counterfeit Lady
The Royal Assassin
The Conspiring Woman
The Detecting Duchess

The Milliner Mysteries
The Killing at Kaldaire House
Murder at the Marlowe Club

The Mystery at Chadwick House

Deadly Village

Kate Parker

JDP Press

This is a work of fiction. All names, characters, and incidents are products of the author's imagination. Any resemblance to actual occurrences or persons, living or dead, is coincidental. Historical events and personages are fictionalized.

Deadly Village

Copyright ©2025 by Kate Parker

All rights reserved. With the exception of brief quotes used in critical articles or reviews, no part of this book may be reproduced in any form or by any means without written permission of the author.

This title claims exemption of EAA because the publisher qualifies as a micro-enterprise.

ISBN: 979-8-9920152-4-9 (ebook)
ISBN: 979-8-9920152-5-6 (print)

Published by JDP Press
Cover Design by Lyndsey Lewellen of Llewellen Designs
Formatting by Bravia Books, LLC

Dedication

For my family, my friends, and anyone who enjoys a good historical mystery.

To John, forever.

England, early March, 1942

Chapter One

Stephen Ronald Redmond, named for his grandfathers, let out a pitiful howl, his tiny face turning red as he lashed out with his fists, and I held him closer in my arms. Even wrapped up, cradled against my body warmth, the poor child was cold.

He had been fine the few days we'd been in hospital, those few days mandated for all newborns and mothers, and the hospital had been warm. Adam managed a few days off to see his son, and Stevie had seemed warm enough then. I certainly had been. But two days after we returned to my father's house, Adam had to return to his army base somewhere in the north.

And then things, such as Stevie's temper, his digestive tract, the weather, the cold in the house, and my father's patience, had gone downhill day by day.

A cold blast from Scotland was making my father's house colder than ever. Stevie was too cold to even eat. He wailed constantly. This had gone on for two days by then. I don't know why I thought of the oven, but I took Stevie to the kitchen, turned on the oven, opened the oven door, set a chair in front of where the heat poured out, and sat with Stevie on my lap.

I thought I'd try to feed him when he and I warmed up a little.

It worked. Stevie had fed as if he was the starving child he was before he dropped off to sleep, warm and content. I only had a few minutes to relax before I tensed as my father entered the room and Stevie started to wail again.

"Doesn't he ever stop?" my father asked me.

"Only when you aren't around."

"What do you mean by that?"

"You shout all the time."

"He cries all the time."

"You fuss at me, I tense up, then Stevie gets upset and he cries. And then you shout and make it worse."

My father looked around the kitchen and started shouting about a new subject. "You can't heat the house with the oven."

"I'm not trying to. I was trying to warm him up enough that he could eat and go to sleep. Which worked until you came in here." To show my point, I turned off the oven and shut the door. Then I glared at my father. I was exhausted and he wasn't helping.

"Do you know how much fuel costs?"

I gave a small shriek and marched off with Stevie in my arms toward the stairs. Upset by my increased tension and sudden movement, Stevie screamed louder.

My father shook his head. "I've contacted Sir Henry. He'll bring the car around in half an hour to drive you two to Esther's."

"I was told not to move the baby or me for six weeks if I could help it. If we weren't bombed out," I told him. We hadn't yet made it halfway there.

And thank goodness, we hadn't been bombed out.

My father's face was nearly as red as Stevie's. "I don't as a rule condone infanticide, but this is too much. He's getting worse, not better. You need to leave."

"It's cold and damp in here and he's uncomfortable. I'm uncomfortable. A short time in front of the oven fixed that." I still felt better from the extra heat.

"It's too expensive."

"He'll get older. The weather will get better. If you could find a little love for him or for me, it wouldn't seem so expensive." I hurried across the hall and up the stairs to my room, fighting tears.

"He's my grandson and someday I'll love him, but I can't take any more of this. Two weeks is all I can handle. I'll send Mrs. Johnson up to help you pack, and I'll help carry things downstairs." My father had followed us. Now he shut the door with a little more force than necessary.

I was being thrown out of my home.

All I could do was join Stevie in a burst of tears.

By the time Sir Henry arrived, Mrs. Johnson had packed up all our clothes and our ration books while I had stopped my tears and dressed us both for the miserable rainy weather. Why couldn't my father have waited for a sunny day, provided we were ever to have one again?

My father, Sir Henry, and Mrs. Johnson ran between the house and the car with our travel cases, umbrellas held at an angle against the wind and rain.

When everything was ready, I thanked Mrs. Johnson for all her help. Then my father held the umbrella to protect us as I carried Stevie to the car. I climbed into the back seat, and with the baby on my lap and both of us wrapped in a blanket, we drove off. My last view of my childhood home was Mrs. Johnson snapping some words at my father, who was looking quite relieved.

"Is Esther all right with us coming out to visit? Does she even know?" I asked as soon as we were down the street.

"She knows and she highly approves. She believes the last thing you need is tension in these early days of motherhood. Bad for you and bad for the little one," Sir Henry said.

With the inclement weather and the lack of petrol, there was no real traffic between my father's house in the London suburbs and Esther's in the village of Chipping Ford in Oxfordshire. I slumped into the back seat and Stevie fell asleep in my arms for the entire trip, his lullaby the constant swish of the windscreen wipers.

If I didn't know better, I would think Stevie was relieved to be away from his grandfather. I certainly was.

When we arrived, Sir Henry held an umbrella up to protect us from the car to the house where everyone was waiting to greet us. They, even nearly five-year-old Johnny and three-year-old Becca, made a fuss over Stevie while Sir Henry carried our cases and the blanket in.

"We have a fire going to warm your room upstairs and we've set up the cradle in there. The room's in the front on the left. The sheets and blankets have been aired and warmed with the warming pans the house came with when my father bought the place just before the war. Go on upstairs and I'll bring you a hot mug of tea," Esther said. "Do you need anything else?"

"I don't know. I don't think so," I said, shaking my head.

Stevie was crying by the time I reached the top of the stairs. All my muscles tensed until I realized children cried in this house all the time and no one fussed. I opened up the door to my room and found it to be the warmest room I'd been in all winter.

After I shed us both of our outerwear, I settled us in the rocking chair in front of the fire and started to feed Stevie. Wonder of wonders, he fed well for the second time that day. By the time Esther appeared with my tea, his eyes had drooped closed.

"This is the best he has eaten and slept since he came

home from the hospital," I whispered, smiling in gratitude.

"No wonder. Your father was tense and his attitude spreads over everybody, making it harder to care for a sensitive infant. I adore your father, but when mine started telling me what he overheard when he visited, we both knew it was only a matter of time until one of you asked for you and the baby to move out here."

"Two weeks. I wonder if that's some sort of record," I said.

"It doesn't matter. You two will be warm and safe here, and by spring, if we ever have a spring, things will look much better."

I studied Esther's expression. "That's when you want me out." I felt tension flood my veins and Stevie began to stir.

"No. You brought your ration book, and we have plenty of room. It will be nice having another adult in the house. I think my father will put you to work writing some sort of column on raising a newborn during the war to give him an excuse to drive out here every couple of weeks."

"Oh! I never thanked your father for the ride out here. With petrol rationing, the drive must have cost him a fortune."

"He was glad to do it, and I was glad he was available to do it," Esther assured me.

"Won't I be an extra guest when James gets leave to see his family?"

"Not any more than I will be when Adam gets leave."

Esther gave me a smile. "We'll work this out. You just worry about keeping this little one fed and warm. I'm across the hall in front. Behind my room is the nursery and then Goldie's room is at the back. Magda is downstairs in the back by the kitchen. It's a big house. My father was brilliant when he chose this place. Now, drink your tea and let us know when you want us to bring up your cases."

"Let me drink my tea and then I'll carry them up."

"No. Enjoy being pampered. In a couple of days, you'll have to start tending your own fire and coming down to meals. We try to be self-sufficient here, but I don't expect you to completely jump in less than three weeks after giving birth." Esther gave me a sunny smile.

"I've forgotten what normal life is, without frozen silences or shouting instead of conversations. Thank you." I drank my tea, feeling warm and relaxed with Stevie sleeping peacefully on my lap while the rain pattered a gentle beat on the windowpanes.

For the first time since Stevie was born, I felt as if we might both survive this.

Chapter Two

As much as I enjoyed eating, planting a vegetable garden was more work than I expected. By the time eight weeks had passed and Easter with it, I had regained my strength and patience and Stevie was beginning to grow, things that would never have happened in my father's house. As spring and sunshine began to win over wintery rain, Esther and I had gone out in our wellies after a local farmer had turned the ground over for us to plant the earliest vegetables.

I bundled up Stevie in the pram that both of Esther's children had previously used and set him in a protected corner so I could keep an ear out for him while working. Johnny and Becca were playing on the village green under the watchful eye of Goldie, their nanny, so we had been able to put in a full hour of uninterrupted work.

"Mrs. Powell! Is it safe to plant this early?" a woman about our age in a tweed skirt and heavy jacket asked from the other side of the fence.

When Esther rose from her crouched position and began to walk over, I followed. "Lady Lydia, how are you?" Esther said as she pulled off her work gloves. Underneath, her skin and nails were perfect. "We can plant the earliest vegetables now. The others we've started in the potting shed."

I left my gloves on and my hands behind me, since my digits were covered with soil, thanks to a few small tears in my gardening gloves.

"Lady Lydia Fletcher, may I present my friend Mrs. Livvy Redmond. She and her baby have come to stay with us for the duration," Esther said.

"Your husband was no doubt in the military?" Lady Lydia asked. Close up, she was a milk-and-honey blonde with lovely skin and nails unmarred by physical work. I had already burned my fingers twice before I learned how to build a fire on my bedroom grate and my face felt as if it was already turning pink from the sun.

"He still is. He was wounded in France, so now he's training troops."

"Mine was an RAF pilot. One of the unlucky ones. Therefore, I'm Lady Lydia, to distinguish me from my mother-in-law, Lady Agatha, also a widow, and my sister-in-law, Lady Jane, also a widow with the newest earl in the form of her baby son. We all live in the lodge below the manor house, just up the rise from the church. The manor house was our home until the Ministry of Defense commandeered it for offices." This last was said with a sniff.

I'd certainly been put in my place. "I'm pleased to meet you. Now that the weather's better, I imagine we'll see each other in church and around the village."

"I daresay we shall. Good day. Good day, Mrs. Powell."

We stood by the fence, Esther pulling her gloves back on, and watched Lady Lydia walk down the edge of the paved lane through the village toward the shop with the post office.

"What was that about?" I asked when she was out of earshot.

"She wanted to establish her status, and yours. Status is very important to Lady Lydia. Lady Jane, the one with the baby son, ordinarily just goes by Jane unless her mother-in-law or sister-in-law are around."

"How old is the baby?" I was more interested in playmates for when Stevie was a little older.

"He was born last Christmas, I think. Four months now, maybe? Yes, four months and a bit more."

We returned to planting. "I never visited Abby during planting season, but I had plenty of practice weeding. I didn't know planting was this hard."

"How is your cousin? And her boys?" Esther asked.

"She and Sir John are fine, and very busy, with all their farmland. Their oldest boy is studying engineering and mathematics at university, courtesy of the Royal Engineers.

The younger three are in school and working on the farm on their holidays. They must be doing the same thing along the south coast that we're doing here."

Esther smiled. "Except we don't have farmland, we have a garden. Thank goodness."

We went back to work, only to be interrupted twenty minutes later by thick dark clouds rolling across the sky and blotting out the sun. I took Stevie inside in his pram and then began to collect the extra gardening tools Esther couldn't manage. Esther put an armload away and then greeted her children and the nanny as they all rushed inside through the side door closest to the garden.

I came out of the shed and started to head toward the house as the first drops of rain began to splatter against the path and the fence. The sound of hurrying feet and a metallic squeak caught my attention. A dark-haired young woman pushing a pram was hurrying past our gate as the rain thickened.

"Quick!" I shouted. "Through the gate. Come this way."

She did, huddling against the back end of the pram. I directed her through the side door and followed on her heels. Once we were in, Esther greeted us with towels. I dried myself off as best I could and said, "I guess you two know each other."

"It is a village," the stranger said with a smile. "Thank you for letting us in. We'd have been completely soaked by the time we reached the lodge."

"Are you Lady Jane?" I asked.

"You must have been talking to Lydia," the woman said, rolling her dark eyes. "I'm Jane, and this is Andrew. I try to avoid the titles when possible. They seem so irrelevant these days."

I leaned over the pram as his mother finished drying off her baby and turned the towel on herself. Andrew was much larger than Stevie and blue eyed, so different from his mother, and with the whitest of blond hair. "What a handsome baby. I'm Livvy. This little guy over here is Stevie. Stephen, actually."

Jane glanced over at my pram. "Two months? He's a little one."

"Yes, ten weeks today, as a matter of fact." I smiled with that devoted, lovesick grin I had whenever I looked at him.

"No wonder I haven't seen you around the village before now. The weather has been too cold and wet for babies. Welcome to Chipping Ford." She held out her hand. The skin was rough from washing and lighting fires, so unlike her sister-in-law's.

I shook it gladly.

Esther and Jane discussed upcoming cooking classes at the Women's Institute and the next meeting of the Mothers' Guild at the village hall. By then, the rain had tapered off to a fine drizzle.

"Come along, Andrew. We should be able to get home now without drowning." Jane bundled him up and they left by the side entrance.

"She seems awfully nice," I said as I took the towels to hang them in the scullery.

"She is," Esther called after me. "Not as worried about status as Lydia."

As I returned, Johnny ran into the hallway, sneezing.

* * *

Nearly five-year-old Johnny passed his cold to three-year-old Becca who passed it to Stevie, which caused me to turn into a bowl of jelly. Stevie cried and gasped and whimpered and couldn't sleep. Goldie, the nanny, found he was teething as well as suffering from a cold and she showed me how to gently rub his gums. She also showed me how to hold him under a tent over a steaming bowl of water to ease his gasping.

I'd had no idea babies could start teething this young or suffer so much. It just reminded me how much I didn't know about being a mother.

After all that didn't get Stevie or me any sleep, I called the local doctor and asked if he'd stop by and check on the baby. He promised to stop by that evening after his surgery and rounds at the cottage hospital.

I'd signed both of us up at Dr. Sampson's surgery when we'd first moved to Chipping Ford, as he was the only doctor in the village, but he hadn't yet seen my Stevie.

"Don't worry, Livvy. You just rub his gums and do the tent thing with the bowl of hot water and he'll probably be better by the time Dr. Sampson arrives," Esther said.

"What if he gets held up? Stevie is so miserable."

"Why don't I take Stevie for an hour and let you take a nap?"

"You have too much on your plate already. I should be able to manage one baby."

It turned out I couldn't. By afternoon, Stevie and I were both reduced to tears. Esther took Stevie and ordered me to bed. After an hour's sleep, I could manage once again, although I felt as if I'd failed.

The doctor arrived after dinner. Dr. Sampson was businesslike, listening to Stevie's chest and back with his stethoscope and looking in his ears and mouth with a light. Stevie was fascinated by the doctor and with his tools and stopped crying. I felt my own tension ease as I sensed the doctor's experience from his graying hair, lines around his mouth and eyes, and confident way he handled Stevie.

"He's early with his teething, which makes it a little harder for him. Won't hurt him, but may make your life a bit rougher. His cold is already lessening." When Dr. Sampson heard what Nanny Goldie had showed me with his gums and the tent, he completely approved.

Then he sat me down with Stevie in my arms and said, "Childhood is much harder on the parents than on the children. This is your first, and everything is new and strange. You have good advisors here in Mrs. Powell and Nanny Goldie. But if you find their advice isn't helping, call me at my surgery."

He gave me a reassuring smile. "Now, I want you to try to relax. Stevie senses when you are worried and it makes him fussy. He feels the tension in your arms when you hold him. Make taking care of him your number one job and getting enough rest yourself next in importance. Esther is sensible. She won't mind if you slack off on your chores to take care of your baby or yourself."

Stevie willingly lay in his cot and I walked Dr. Sampson downstairs. He used a cane, but he struggled so much I thought he should use two. I suspected he only used one so he could carry his Gladstone medical bag in his other hand. When we reached the ground floor, he turned kindly blue eyes on me.

"You and Stevie are going to be fine. And it will get easier as you become more certain of yourself. As you get used to being a mother."

There was a knock on the front door and I walked over to answer it. Esther came out into the hallway to say goodbye to the doctor as I discovered Constable Bell on our front step. It was still light out, so I wasn't worried about breaking blackout regulations.

"How can I help you, Constable?"

"It's the doctor I need."

"Yes, Bell?" For the first time, I heard weariness in the doctor's voice. It must have been a long day for him before he arrived at Esther's house.

"It's Mrs. Bryant. She's dead. Murdered. I don't know what to do. I've never handled a murder before. People don't get murdered here." The uniformed bobby looked into each of our faces as if they'd contain clues.

"That's easy, Constable," I said with confidence. "Call the doctor, which you did. Make sure no one traipses through the crime scene. Take photographs of anything that might be important. If it's indoors, lock up the room if you can't lock up the whole building. Check around the…"

For the first time, I saw the doctor frown. The constable's mouth had dropped open.

"How do you know all that?" Bell said, his eyes widening.

"Before the baby came, I was a reporter for the London *Daily Premier* newspaper. I saw a lot of murder scenes." This was an easier answer than explaining my work for Sir Malcolm Fremantle, which I couldn't divulge without breaking the Official Secrets Act.

"I don't have a camera."

"Livvy, get your camera and go with Bell and the doctor. Help the constable out," Esther said. "You know you want to."

"Stevie…"

"Between Nanny Goldie and me, Stevie will be fine. Don't worry. Just get your camera and go."

I looked at the two men who stood watching me. With a nod, I hurried upstairs to our room. Tiptoeing around, I got my hat, coat, gloves, camera bag, and a notebook and pencil. With a final gaze at Stevie, I hurried back downstairs. "He's asleep for the moment. If he—"

"Go," Esther said and pointed out the door.

I followed the doctor outside, where Bell was waiting. We all piled into the doctor's car and drove the short distance to what I guessed was Mrs. Bryant's cottage.

There was still enough light that I could make out the cottage I'd noticed before. A vine growing along the fence by the street was currently covered with buds. Another vine grew over a trellis near the front door, also coming to life, this one in rose-buds. There was a window on either side of the entrance to the golden-stone-built house, with a thatched roof pitched steeply enough to provide a room or two upstairs in the attic. Two chimneys rose above the roof on either side of the door.

As we climbed out of the car, I readied my camera. "Was the door open when you first saw the cottage, Constable?"

"Yes. That's why I investigated."

I asked Dr. Sampson to wait a moment while I took a picture showing the door ajar and another of the doorstep with no sign of footprints. Then I waved him ahead of me.

He pushed the door fully open and disappeared to the left. I followed, Bell bringing up the rear, and saw the doctor had gone into the drawing room. A table lamp was on, the blackout curtain covering the window. A woman, perhaps in her fifties or sixties, was slumped in an overstuffed chair facing the door with a large knife handle sticking out of her chest. Blood stained her white blouse and blue cardigan, but very little had fallen on her gray skirt.

"Can you wait a moment, Doctor? I assume you don't see any signs of life?" I asked.

He felt around her neck and jaw and then said, "No signs of life" as he backed up.

I took a few photographs of the woman, the chair, and the knife without moving anything while the doctor and the constable waited for me. I was on my knees, taking a photo from below the level of the knife when I heard a man's voice call out, "Hello? Mrs. Bryant?"

Chapter Three

I turned in time to see a plumpish, middle-aged man, balding on top, stop in the entrance to the drawing room and say, "Good grief."

I immediately looked to see if he had any blood on his gray three-piece suit, but I didn't see any.

Constable Bell stepped forward to block the other man's path as he said, "Aren't you Mrs. Bryant's lodger? Working up at the manor house?"

"Yes. Howard MacDonald." They shook hands.

"How long have you resided here?" The constable had his notebook out, and I decided it was time for me to get back to my task.

Once I had taken photos of her from every direction, I then began to photograph the fireplace, the walls with the windows, the pictures on the walls, and the doorway. The chair where the victim sat was at a distance from a sofa, with end tables holding lamps by each. I couldn't tell about the chair, but the fabric on the sofa looked unworn.

While I worked, I listened to the constable's questions and learned Mr. MacDonald was a civilian employee, in charge of a small office in the manor house where his work was covered by the Official Secrets Act, and had been living with Mrs. Bryant two months.

"Anything else you want a photo of, Constable?" I broke in.

"Is that a drop of blood?" Dr. Sampson asked, pointing at the rug between the chair and the doorway.

I took a photo of the spot and then said, "How far do you think that is from Mrs. Bryant?" as I pulled out my own notebook and pencil from my coat pocket. "That is Mrs. Bryant?"

"Aye," said the constable. "Distance of maybe four feet."

"And here's another one on the floorboard, maybe another four feet farther along." I snapped another photo and then took notes describing all the shots I'd taken. "How did the blood drops get there? Do you think the killer was injured?"

"It would make life easier if he were," Bell replied.

"If she were stabbed here, by the door," Mr. MacDonald said, "then walked or was forced back to the chair, it might explain the drops of blood."

"You think the killer wasn't marked by Mrs. Bryant or her blood?" Dr. Sampson asked.

"No reason why they should be, if they shoved the knife in and didn't pull back at all. The damage could all be internal. If the knife was held at arm's length from the killer, there would be room for a few drops of blood to fall to the floor," Mr. MacDonald said. He had a serious look on his face, as if he were picturing the assault.

"Or the killer just let go and let Mrs. Bryant stumble backward to fall into the chair," I added. I looked around. "Any other photographs I should take in here?"

"That's a very nice camera," Dr. Sampson said.

"My husband gave it to me after we learned I was carrying his child, so I could take pictures of the baby and send them to him. He was already stationed away from here and he was afraid he'd never see Stevie."

"Do you have any photos of Stevie on this film?" Dr. Sampson asked me and then looked pointedly at Constable Bell.

"Yes, four. Plus I still have more shots available on this roll of film."

"The police in Oxford will want to develop that, but they'll give you the pictures of your son. They should give you another roll of film, too. Never know when we may need your talents again, Mrs. Redmond," the constable said.

"I'm surprised you know my name," I said. I was surprised because with Stevie, I hadn't been out of the house much during the cold, rainy weather we'd had since I arrived.

"I make it a point to. Necessary in my job."

"Glad to know, Constable. Anything else I should take a photo of?"

"I don't know."

"What was she doing in that chair?" I asked.

Constable Bell looked puzzled. Dr. Sampson studied the woman in her chair for a moment and then nodded. "No books or papers on the table next to the lamp, although it's turned on. The radio along the wall there is turned off. No sign of a cup of tea, and I know Mrs. Bryant was fond of a cuppa. She worked for me and my predecessor part-time for years."

"If she was stabbed in the doorway and staggered backward to fall into the chair, there wouldn't be any reason for her to be sitting there," MacDonald said. "She just stumbled backward, away from her killer."

I took another photo of the table and jotted a few more notes in my book, while Mr. MacDonald asked, "Does she still work for you?"

"No. I retired her a few months ago," the doctor said. "I hated to do it, lord knows she said she needed the money often enough, but she was getting further and further behind on her work and my practice was suffering as a result. The patients have to come first."

"That's right. I talked to a Mrs. Hunter when I signed up at your surgery." And that had been over two months before.

"Yes. She's been a godsend. She's not the gossip Mrs. Bryant was and much more efficient." The doctor looked around. "I don't see anything else. I wonder why she was sitting in here and not the kitchen."

"She'd know I'd be home soon for my dinner. So she might have waited for her cuppa until I returned. That is, if she were just murdered. Was she just murdered, Doctor?" Mr. MacDonald asked.

Dr. Sampson nodded, still studying the victim in silence.

"She probably had a visitor." As soon as I spoke, I frowned. "Of course, she did. And her visitor killed her." I went out to the kitchen in the back of the house, the constable following me.

"She wasn't heating the kettle." I touched it gingerly. "It's not even warm." I took a couple of photos of the kitchen, including one of the stove and kettle. There were no dishes in the sink or in the drying rack, and I took a photo of that too.

Then I checked the oven. It was on and Mr. MacDonald's dinner was in a pan, looking slightly dried out. I turned off the stove and pulled the dinner out before I took a photo of it.

"Constable, will I be able to eat my dinner and sleep in my bed tonight?" Mr. MacDonald asked.

The constable looked shocked, but then said, "You can eat your dinner if you do it quickly, but you'll have to find another place to sleep tonight."

Mr. MacDonald found a plate and silverware, dished up his dinner, and turned on the kettle as if he was completely familiar with the kitchen, which made sense if he'd lived there for two months. He sat in one particular highbacked slatted wooden chair at the kitchen table as if he habitually sat there.

I couldn't imagine how Mr. MacDonald could eat, knowing there was a dead body in the next room, but I guessed he was very hungry.

"Whoever her guest was, she wasn't giving them tea," Dr. Sampson said from the doorway.

"Constable, have you made certain there is no one hiding in the cottage?" I asked.

Bell looked around wide-eyed. "No."

"That is the next thing you need to do. Your inspector will ask that," I told him.

"Oh." He walked upstairs and then back and forth, and we could follow the sound of his footsteps in every room.

"You're very good to do this for him," Dr. Sampson told me.

"I don't care for the idea of a killer loose in Chipping Ford. I live here. My baby lives here. My friend and her children live here."

The doctor nodded.

I turned to lock the back door and stopped.

"What is it?"

"The back door is unlocked." I picked up my camera and

shot another photo.

The constable came back into the kitchen. "No one here."

"The back door is unlocked," I told him.

"Well, you'd expect that in any of the cottages around here. People don't lock their doors," the constable told me.

"Something the killer was counting on?" I asked.

"Then why leave the front door ajar?" he asked me.

I shrugged. It seemed as if the killer had made a mistake.

When Mr. MacDonald finished his dinner, he washed up and left the dishes to dry in the rack. Then the constable went upstairs with him while he packed a bag to take with him for the night.

The constable locked the back door and then followed us out, locking the front door after us.

"At least there weren't any open windows," the doctor said in a jovial tone.

"You agree, Constable?" I asked.

"Aye."

I made a note of that, too.

"But she kept her bedroom messier than I would have thought," he continued.

The doctor and I looked at each other. "Unlock the door, Constable."

We piled back into the house followed by Mr. MacDonald, and the constable led us to the right. As we were under blackout regulations, as soon as the doctor turned on the ceiling light, the constable and I closed the blackout curtains in the ground-floor bedroom instantly, by habit.

"This is Mrs. Bryant's room?" I asked Mr. MacDonald, who was loitering in the hallway and carefully not touching anything.

"Yes."

I took photos of the slightly open drawers in the dresser with clothes peeking out and the doors to the wardrobe ajar. The bed was also slightly unmade. Once I made notes of what these photos were of, we again left the house and the constable locked it behind us.

Then the doctor drove all four of us to the Chipping Ford police constabulary house. It was a stone cottage with the entrance to the police constabulary on the left by a notice board and an entrance to Constable Bell's living quarters on the right. We entered the left-hand door and I took the film out of my camera and the pages out of my notebook that corresponded with the photos while Constable Bell and the doctor were on the telephone to the police headquarters in Oxford.

Whoever answered in Oxford listened to Bell's concise account over the phone, helped by my suggestions, and then after hearing Dr. Sampson's report, must have told Bell to hand the body over to the mortuary to await the coroner and that an inspector would be out in the morning to take over the investigation. The constable looked deflated when he told us his orders.

"Call Maudie Elliott now and see if she wants to pick up the body tonight," Dr. Sampson said.

As Bell returned to the telephone, I said, "The funeral director here is a woman?"

"And quite good. She took over the business when her husband died, but she'd been doing most of the work for ages before that," the doctor said.

The constable hung up the phone and said, "She'll meet us at the cottage in an hour."

We left the police constabulary house, Bell leaving the door unlocked, and the doctor went out to his car. "I'll park at my house and then walk over."

Bell responded with a wave.

"May I walk you home, Mrs. Redmond?" Mr. MacDonald asked.

"Thank you, but shouldn't you be finding another place to stay the night? I don't think Constable Bell will let you go back into Mrs. Bryant's house."

"I'm sure I can find a spot to bed down in the manor house. Then tomorrow I'll get the billeting office to find me a new place."

"Do you have a family who wants to join you?" I asked.

"No. I'm a widower. One daughter lives with her family in Canada, and the other lives with hers in York. I'm on my own now, so any old billet will do. Your husband. Is he in the army?"

"He's a major in a training brigade. He was wounded in France. I was able to see him for a few days after Stevie was born." I took a few more steps. "Are you a policeman?"

"Why do you ask that?"

"You ate your dinner in the next room from a dead body, and you found a logical reason for those blood drops to be on the floor."

He smiled. "I have a strong stomach."

We walked down the lane to the Old Vicarage where I lived with Esther. It was full dark now and our voices sounded loud against the sounds of the night creatures. No doubt a few curtains twitched. He waited just inside the gate while I opened the door and went in. I waved to him, said "Thank you," and shut the door.

The door when I arrived home was unlocked, but everyone was asleep. I stood there for a moment, listening to the difference between what I heard now and what I'd heard at Mrs. Bryant's. Even with everyone asleep, there were little sounds here that hadn't been in Mrs. Bryant's cottage. Hers held the silence of death. Here a bed creaked as someone turned over. One of the children cried out in their sleep. Someone snored.

I locked the door and tiptoed up the stairs. I put down my camera gear and notebook without turning on a light and, as my eyes adapted to the dark, crept over to Stevie's cot. He shifted and sniffled in his sleep and I marveled at how incredibly adorable he was. I undressed and climbed into bed, knowing it would be a short night's sleep.

* * *

Stevie awoke me demanding to be fed while it was still dark out. His needs met, we both lay down for what little sleep we would get before the rest of the household rose.

As it turned out, Stevie was as tired as I was and we were both asleep again when there was a gentle tapping on my door, followed by Esther coming into my room. She glanced into Stevie's cot first before coming to the side of my bed and whispering, "Constable Bell and an Inspector Grimsby are here for you. What did you do?"

"Nothing," I said, wiping the sleep from my eyes and sitting up.

"I'll tell them you'll be down in a moment." Esther slipped out so I could throw on the clothes from the evening before and talk to the policemen.

When I went downstairs, I found Grimsby lived up to his name. He was nearly a head taller than Bell and much thinner, with a hairless crown. He wore what appeared to be a perpetual frown etched deeply into the lines of his face. "Mrs. Redmond?" His voice was frosty.

"Yes."

"Come with us, please."

"I can't. I have to feed the baby and then ask Esther to watch him for me."

"This is a murder inquiry. Come with us now." Grimsby glared at me, sounding as if he were trying out for the

Gestapo.

"After I feed my baby." I turned to Bell. "I'll meet you at the constabulary house as soon as I finish."

"And bring your camera," Grimsby said.

"Why? You have the film."

"Just bring it. And hurry up." Grimsby turned on his heel and marched away.

He sounded as if he wanted to arrest me.

Chapter Four

"What an unpleasant man," Esther said.

"His life is in Oxford. I'm sure he didn't want to be dragged out here to the countryside," I said. "I'm going to feed and change Stevie, but then I'll need you to watch him for me while I talk to the police."

"Why? What's going on?"

I told her, and it was more than an hour before I finally reached the police constabulary. I walked in the door and was immediately greeted by Grimsby with "It took you long enough."

"Caring for a baby is more complex than you seem to realize. Now, why did you want to see my camera?"

"Do you have film in it?"

"Not currently."

He proceeded to ask me about every dial and switch, how to put the film in and take it out, and how I had taken the various photographs. When he finished, I asked, "When will I get the first four shots on the roll?"

"The first four shots?"

"They're of my son, to be mailed to his father. When you develop the roll, I want the first four shots, which will mean nothing to you. I also request to have my film replaced by a fresh roll so I can take more photographs of Stevie."

"Agreed. Now, these notes. What are they referring to?"

"They are what the photos are of, in order. When you have them developed, we can go over them together with the list and I can clarify anything that isn't clear from the photographs alone."

"We should have the prints sent out here late this afternoon."

"Then I don't imagine you'll need me until then." I turned to go.

"I need a statement."

"About what?" I looked at him in confusion.

"How did you end up at the dead woman's cottage?"

"Dr. Sampson had just finished seeing my son when Constable Bell came to the door, saying he needed the doctor because Mrs. Bryant had been killed. He asked the doctor what steps he was supposed to take, since he'd never been called to a murder before." I looked hard at Inspector Grimsby. "People don't murder each other out here."

"What does that have to do with you?" Grimsby appeared annoyed that I had wandered off the topic.

"I was a London reporter and I've seen the police deal with lots of murders, so I told him what steps to take. He didn't have a camera, so I brought mine, and a notebook to write down what each of the photos was of."

"Even though your own son was ill."

I felt my face heat. "It turns out a good deal of his problem was teething, and Esther and Nanny Goldie had already taught me how to handle that. Stevie was asleep when I left, and asleep when I returned."

Grimsby snapped his notepad shut and said, "That will do for now. We'll let you know when the photos come in the mail."

"Until later, then." I picked up my camera and left the constabulary, returning home.

The rest of the day was spent feeding me, feeding Stevie, and working in the garden and the potting shed. Once again, Stevie took up his position in his pram in a sheltered place where he could get sunlight and fresh air without getting chilled.

At the warmest part of the day, Jane came by pushing Andrew in his pram. Her brown eyes, her best feature, smiled. "It's lovely today. Come take a walk with me."

I glanced at Esther.

"Go on. We're about done."

With a smile, I leaped up and said, "I'll be right there." I stripped off my gloves, washed my hands and face in the cloakroom, grabbed a hat and gloves, and returned to push

Stevie out onto the lane.

Andrew was propped up, enjoying the sights, while Stevie slept on. "He's three months now?" Jane asked.

"Nearly. And Andrew?"

"Five months."

I tried to phrase my next question as delicately as I could. "What happened to his father, that he is Lord Andrew?"

"He's buried in the churchyard over there. He made it home." Jane took a deep breath and blinked twice. "He was shot down during a bombing raid and made it back to crash land in Britain. He survived to make it to hospital, but that was it. Where's your husband?"

"Somewhere in Britain, training soldiers. He was shot up in France and made it back, but he'll always walk with crutches or canes." I shrugged.

Jane gave me a watery smile. "Who'd have thought the army would be safer than the RAF?"

"Was he a pilot before the war?" I was curious. "Adam was already an army officer before I met him."

"Yes, but just little cloth two-seaters. But he loved it."

"How long were you married?"

"Peter and I were married at the beginning of the war before he went to flight training. He survived the Battle of Britain, only to go down in a bombing raid after the end of the Blitz. So, less than two years by the calendar. Actual time spent together? Perhaps a month."

"I understand that feeling," I told her.

"How are you enjoying living here in the village?" It was her turn to sound curious.

"I've lived in London all my life, so this is different. It's very pretty and quiet. No bombing. It's good for Stevie. Of course, I'm used to lots of traffic noises, petrol fumes, underground trains rumbling. Here it's just a horse cart passing now and again and fresh air."

"Esther brought a lot of experienced help with her, so that must help you as a new mother, too."

"Says the lady of the manor," I said with a smile.

She stopped then and looked at me. "We're in the lodge, not the manor, which has been taken over by the MOD. And I got more help from Esther and Goldie and Magda than I've ever received from my mother-in-law and sister-in-law. My sister-in-law has never had children. And we just have some daily help from the village. So, don't give me this 'lady of the manor' nonsense."

"Jane, I'm sorry. I didn't know things had been so bad for you. Esther has been a blessing for me, too. And for her help, as you call them. She guaranteed jobs for both Goldie and Magda just before the war started so they could escape Germany. They were her third set of help she brought over before the war."

"They're Jewish refugees."

"Yes. Goldie came over with her sons and Magda's son and daughter had made it to America in the mid-1930s. And we're lucky to have them both with us. Plus Esther has hired cleaning help in the village for a couple of hours a week for the heavy cleaning."

"We have Mrs. Anderson in daily to clean the lodge and Mrs. Coffey comes in to cook our dinner every day. She's a better cook than any of us." Jane looked embarrassed by her admission. "But what brought you out here with such a young baby?"

"Safety." I stopped talking for a moment and decided to tell her the whole story. "My father threw me out of the house when Stevie was two weeks old."

"Good heavens. Why?"

"He cried. Made noise."

Jane stared at me as we walked down the middle of the lane. "Where were you living before he was born?"

"With my father. My flat was blown up at the end of the Blitz. Since my father had an entire house to himself in the outskirts of London, I was far down the list for available flats and so I lived with him until—he threw us out. And Esther has been my best friend since school days."

"Esther's a great neighbor to have. We're both very lucky to know her."

"How did it feel living in the manor house at the beginning of the war? And how did it happen that you had the lodge to move into when the Ministry of Defense moved into the manor house?"

"Ah." Jane smiled. "A little history. The manor house is

huge. It easily takes a staff of twenty to keep it running, as Lydia will tell you if you ask. It's also extremely expensive to maintain, and I hope to sell it for Andrew's sake when the MOD move out. The lodge was built for a dowager countess in Victorian times. It's huge and dark and impossible to heat, but it's a hundred times better to live in than the manor house."

We walked in silence to the other end of the village. As we turned around and started back, I asked, "What sort of woman was Mrs. Bryant?"

"You've heard she's dead?" Jane asked.

"I went with Constable Bell to take photographs of the crime scene for him."

"Poor Constable Bell. He's lived in the village all his life, but he had to try to get into the police force twice, finally getting in not long before the war started. Not much experience, and now to handle a murder inquiry. How is he holding up?"

"There's now an Inspector Grimsby running the investigation."

Jane nodded. "Is Bell embarrassed that someone else has taken over?"

"A little, but I think he's secretly relieved," I told her. "I know I would be."

"Good." She was quiet for a moment and then said, "My mother-in-law had some kind of history with Mrs. Bryant, and by history, I mean maybe thirty years ago."

"Do you know what?"

"No. Neither Mrs. Bryant nor Lady Agatha ever said. I had the feeling it had something to do with Lydia's husband, Matthew. Lord Matthew, really. My father-in-law died while I was dating Peter. In 1938. Mr. Bryant had died many years earlier. It was then that Lady Agatha and Mrs. Bryant, who'd been friends since Edward VII was on the throne, had a falling-out. About the rent on Mrs. Bryant's cottage, maybe?"

"It would have been Lord Matthew, Lady Lydia's husband, who would have decided on Mrs. Bryant's rent. Am I right?" I asked.

"I think so. It's the only thing that makes sense."

"Tell me, Jane, what type of a person was Mrs. Bryant?" Learning about her temperament and interests might help us find her killer.

"I always had the feeling she was watching me. Not just me, everyone." Jane shivered at the memory.

"I learned last night that she had worked in Dr. Sampson's surgery. I can't imagine that was a good job for her if she was overly curious about everyone," I told her.

"Dr. Sampson replaced her the beginning of the year. She was furious and gave him a piece of her mind, but he stood firm. Someone said they heard him tell her 'that it wouldn't do.'"

"'That it wouldn't do,'" I repeated.

"Yes. So, he fired her and hired Mrs. Hunter, who lives

on South End Farm," Jane said. "He's had no complaints about her as he had with Mrs. Bryant. She was unreliable. Gossiping about patients and not answering the telephone."

"It sounds as if Mrs. Bryant made a great number of enemies. Constable Bell will have his hands full figuring out who killed her." I was glad I'd offered to take the photographs.

Jane shook her head. "She was a silly woman. Tragic, really. People are already guessing who hated her enough to kill her."

"Anyone guessing your mother-in-law?"

"I doubt it. Everyone still sees her as the lady of the manor. Thank goodness. I never wanted that job." Jane sped up a little.

I glanced down at Andrew, propped up in his pram and surveying his village. "You've got it, whether you wanted it or not."

"I thought Lydia would inherit the title and I'd be safe from all that. Instead, I'm facing two sets of death duties, Matthew's and Peter's, while Lydia wanders around saying 'You can't sell that, it's part of the Fletcher heritage. You'll break Agatha's heart.'" Jane did a fair imitation of Lydia's upper-class accent.

"Would it? Break her heart?" I didn't think Lady Agatha was silly.

"I don't know. Matthew and Peter managed to pay off their father's death duties, so she didn't have to deal with it.

Now we have two sets, one right after the other, and the rates have gone even higher, and she acts as if they don't exist."

I wondered who she meant by "she." I guessed Lydia, since Agatha seemed a little more sensible to me.

We reached the house. Esther had already gone inside and the street seemed empty. "Would you care to come in? I know I could kill for a cup of tea about now."

Jane smiled, and her ordinary face was transfixed into beauty. "I'd love to."

We went inside and shed heavy sweaters and hats from ourselves and blankets from the babies. Esther's cook, Magda, told us she was getting the kettle ready and to go into the drawing room. We found Esther busily knitting, and she and Jane began discussing children's clothing patterns.

The tea was weak but warming. I listened to the other two women talk with half my mind while I considered what Jane had told me. Mrs. Bryant collected enemies, including Jane's mother-in-law, who had been the lady of the manor, and Dr. Sampson. Who else might have it in for her?

Anyone she might have spied on.

When we heard a knock at the door, I opened it to find Constable Bell. "Grimsby has the photographs that you took. They arrived about ten minutes ago."

I glanced at the clock in the hall. "We have half an hour, and then my baby is going to demand his dinner. Understood?"

"Yes, ma'am."

I left Stevie with Esther, explained where I was going, and put on my outdoor wear to follow Constable Bell up the hill to the constabulary house.

Grimsby was sitting behind Bell's desk in the one-room office. "Before we go over these photos, I want to go over your statement again."

"You have twenty-five minutes. Use it the best way you can."

He stared at me without speaking for a moment before he said, "Dr. Sampson was at your house before Constable Bell arrived."

"Yes. He was there about twenty minutes to half an hour."

"Did you see anyone outside on the lane or by the fence when you let him in?"

"I didn't let him in. Esther or Goldie did, I imagine."

"Goldie. She's German, isn't she?"

"She's also Jewish, which is why she's here."

"Does she have any family in England?"

"A son in boarding school and a son in the British army. Twenty minutes."

He stared at me again without speaking. Finally, he pulled out the photos and spread them on the desk. I pulled out the first four, which were of Stevie, and put them in my pocket. My notes were also sitting on the desk, and using them, I put the other photos in order.

"Did Dr. Sampson give you a time of death?" I asked.

"Between seven and eight last evening. Constable Bell saw her door was ajar at eight-ten."

"I wonder who was the last person to see her in her garden," I said. "She obviously spent a great deal of time there to have such a lovely garden."

"We'll follow up," he assured me. "Do you see anything unusual in these photographs?"

"A woman with a knife sticking out of her chest?"

"Now who's wasting time?"

I looked the photos over carefully. "She doesn't appear to have any reason to be sitting in her drawing room. No tea, no newspaper, no knitting."

"I'm talking about the quality of the photos."

"I wish I could say it's my talent, but it was good lighting in her cottage and my husband bought me a very nice camera to take pictures of the baby to send to him."

"Are you certain he bought the camera?"

"Of course, I'm certain he bought it. And I even have the sales receipt."

"Pending further inquiry, I'm confiscating the camera."

"No, you're not. And I'm going home to feed my baby."

As I rose, he barked, "Sit down, Mrs. Redmond."

Chapter Five

"No. I'm going home to feed my baby. Come down later and I'll show you the sales receipt for the camera." I marched out of the police constabulary and down the lane.

I was halfway home before Inspector Grimsby caught up with me. "Stop, Mrs. Redmond."

"I'm going home to feed my baby, Inspector. If you do anything to interfere with that, I will scream this village down, and there will be plenty of witnesses to your cruelty to an infant."

"I have no intention to be cruel to any child, but I do need to see the sales receipt. We have a report that it was stolen."

"It's not the only Leica in England." I continued down the lane at a quick pace, walking into Esther's house with Grimsby on my heels. "I need to feed Stevie," I said to Esther, my teeth clenched. "Could I please get you to show the inspector my sales receipt for the camera while I do that?"

I picked up Stevie, who was fussing, and went upstairs, Esther behind me. I pulled the receipt from the box and handed it to her. "He doesn't get to keep this. He's already accused me of stealing the camera."

"Don't worry. You just feed that little fellow. I'll take care of the inspector," Esther said with an edge to her voice.

"Thank you."

By the time Stevie and I had settled down so he could eat his fill, Esther returned with the receipt. "He's gone. What an obnoxious official. Constable Bell had reversed the digits he'd written down for your camera, although I did point out that is from the most prestigious camera shop in London. They have a royal warrant, and they don't care to have their customers treated as if they are criminals."

I disturbed Stevie with my laughter, and he began to kick. Once I had him settled, I put the receipt away. After we had supper, I sat down to write Adam a letter sending him some of the photos I had of Stevie and an explanation of how the camera had been used and how we'd had a murder in our village.

* * *

The next morning, after everyone had time to feed chickens and children, was the regularly scheduled Women's Institute meeting. Esther left Johnny and Becca playing with Nanny Goldie and I put Stevie in the pram to take him along, stopping by the post office first. Just before I put my letter to Adam on the counter, I held it tightly in my hand and sent him a wish-prayer for safety and good health.

The WI meeting was held in the town hall, a stone-walled building constructed on a slope in the last years of Queen Victoria's reign. It was built on two levels, the larger being the auditorium on the lower side and the upper side holding the stage and a few small rooms used for storage or dressing rooms. Esther had warned me to dress us both warmly, since the building was never heated.

The auditorium was about half full when we arrived with women standing or sitting in small groups, a few of them pushing prams as I was. This was my first WI meeting in Chipping Ford and I had no idea what to expect.

"Is it assigned seating?" I asked, having just spotted Jane and Andrew.

"No. Oh, hello. Did you try that shepherd's pie recipe they were passing around?" Esther said to a woman about our age, wearing a tweed suit and stout shoes, whom I'd seen around before.

"Mrs. Redmond," a commanding voice behind me said, "You need to come over and meet my mother-in-law."

"Oh. Ah. Lady Lydia. Of course." I followed her the length of the auditorium to the front facing the stage where an older woman was seated talking to the two gray-haired women on either side of her. When I reached them, all three stopped talking and turned to stare at me.

They were dressed nearly identically in tweed suits, narrow-brimmed hats, and stout-heeled shoes. They were all thin, as we all were in the days of rationing, and I didn't think I'd ever be able to tell them apart.

"Lady Agatha, Mrs. Withins, Mrs. Brown-Dunn, may I present Mrs. Olivia Redmond. Olivia, this is my mother-in-law, Lady Agatha, and two of her friends, Mrs. Withins and Mrs. Brown-Dunn."

I had no idea which lady was which. The nearest one said, "What a handsome baby. Is it a boy?"

"Yes. His name is Stephen."

"His father is in the military?" the other one asked.

"Yes." I glanced over at Jane. Lady Jane, I reminded myself. "If you'll excuse me?"

Without waiting for a reply, I pushed Stevie away from the women and over to where Jane sat along a side aisle.

"May we join you?"

"Of course. Been checked out by my mother-in-law and her coven?"

Jane was smiling, which made me feel free to grin. "Coven?" I asked quietly.

Her grin widened. "Watch out. The main point of today's meeting will be to find out what happened to the local WI secretary."

"Who is that?"

"Mrs. Bryant, who thought of herself as part of the coven." Her smile told me there was no malice in her words.

"Jane, I don't know when to take you seriously."

"Mrs. Bryant did think of herself as a special friend of

Lady Agatha, although whether or not my mother-in-law thought of her in the same terms is questionable. And everyone is going to want to find out what happened to her."

"They're going to have to talk to Constable Bell," I told her, and I meant it.

Two young farmers' wives came over to join us with their babies. I made a fuss over their babies, who were a little older, and showed off Stevie, who slept through the encounter. I glanced over and saw Esther sat not far away with the mothers of some children who looked the same age as hers.

The meeting was gaveled to order and Stevie stirred, but then settled down again. We all turned our attention to the stage, where a middle-aged woman in yet another tweed suit said, "I call this meeting to order. The first order of business, in light of the death of our friend and secretary, Mrs. Phyllis Bryant, is to elect a new secretary."

"Point of order," a woman in the middle of the room said, rising. "We need to make a formal statement of appreciation for all of Mrs. Bryant's service to the Women's Institute."

"We can't do that until we have a secretary to write it down," the chair said. "Now, do we have any nominees?"

"The chair is Mrs. Frances Otterfield, the wife of the local butcher," Jane whispered quietly.

They finally decided on another middle-aged woman in

a tweed suit and then began their flowery tributes to Mrs. Bryant. After a long and heated debate on whether the WI was "bereaved" or "sorrowful," sorrowful won. Then came the debate on whether they were "sorrowful" or "immensely sorrowful."

At that point, I lost interest entirely and noticed that most of the women speaking wore tweed suits. I felt horribly underdressed in my dress and cardigan. I was called back to the meeting when I heard my name mentioned.

"Mrs. Redmond, report please on what you saw at Mrs. Bryant's last Wednesday evening." I realized I was being addressed by the chair of the meeting, Mrs. Otterfield.

"No." I spoke in a small voice. Jane looked ready to burst out laughing.

"What was that?" the chair demanded. She reminded me of the head of St. Agnes.

"No, I can't. Sorry. It's a police matter." One of the other babies' mother patted me on the shoulder in solidarity.

"If it was a police matter, what were you doing there?"

"You might ask Constable Bell," I suggested.

I looked over at Esther, expecting her to be furious. She appeared to be fighting giggles, as did the ladies with her.

"Well, if you have nothing else to report…?"

I smiled at her apologetically and shook my head.

"Then, Mrs. Sutton, if you'll give your report on root vegetable production in the area this spring?"

I heard a few muffled groans, but when Mrs. Sutton, in

a flowered dress and shapeless sweater, began her report, I understood why. It wasn't that they were disappointed in not hearing from me, they wanted to avoid a report even more unpalatable than the subject.

From there we went to meatless recipes and then the speakers for the next WI meeting. The meeting ended when the vicar came in and gave a benediction and a prayer for a quick victory and safety for all.

Then began the sound of chairs scraping on the wooden floor. One of the other babies' mothers told me "Well done." Jane gave me a smile. Other women, none of whom I knew, but most of them near my age, congratulated me. "Not that I wouldn't love to hear the answer, mind," one said with a laugh.

I pushed Stevie over to Esther at the end of the wave of women when Mrs. Otterfield and Lady Lydia came up to me. "That was not an appropriate answer, young lady," the chair said. "This is your first meeting. Do you intend to go on being rude?"

"That was hardly rude, Frances. You know no one can tell what is going on in a police investigation," Jane said, coming up behind me.

"She's hardly a police officer," Frances, the chair, said.

"But in this case, I have to obey them and do my civic duty. You do believe in doing your civic duty. Of course, you do. I was doing exactly the same as you would in my position," I told her.

"Lady Agatha still wants to know," Lady Lydia said.

"Then have her go up to the police constabulary house and ask Constable Bell. I'm sure he'll tell her anything he is allowed to," I said.

"Then why didn't you?" Lady Lydia demanded.

"Because, not being the police, I don't know what can be told and what can't. You have to ask them."

"But she's Lady Agatha," Lydia exclaimed.

"Who is 'them'?" demanded Frances.

"Constable Bell and Inspector Grimsby," I told her.

"Who is Inspector Grimsby?" Lady Lydia asked in an interrogative tone.

"A detective sent in from Oxford to investigate."

"Investigate what?" Lady Lydia demanded.

"That's what you need to ask the police. Call in at the constabulary house and talk to them."

Esther stepped in before I found myself in more hot water. "We need to get back before Stevie decides it's lunchtime."

"You're right. He can be quite persistent when he's hungry," I agreed. I pushed the pram up the aisle and outside at a good speed, Esther following.

When we arrived at Esther's, I went to feed Stevie while she put the latch on the front door and went to ask when lunch would be ready.

We had finished a luncheon of roasted veggies with a side of spring lettuce when there was a knock on the front door. I went to answer it, guessing it had something to do with this morning's discussion.

I was right.

Constable Bell stood there with his helmet on. "The inspector wants to talk to you at the constabulary. He's had a contingent from the WI asking questions about the death of Phyllis Bryant."

"Of course, he did. I wasn't about to tell them anything."

"How did they find out about him?" he asked.

"That was the one thing I did tell them. That he was in charge of the investigation and they should talk to him. He could decide what they could or couldn't be told." When I saw the surprised expression on the constable's face, I added, "I'll get my hat and gloves."

I did, tiptoeing in and out of our room so I wouldn't wake Stevie, and then telling Esther where I was off to. She laughed when she heard about the "contingent."

"At least I didn't say 'coven,'" I told her.

Shutting the front door behind me, I listened to the bird calls and insects buzzing as we walked up the lane. The weather was warming under a clear sky that afternoon. "Was he angry because I told them he was in the village, or because I hadn't told them anything else?"

"He's not convinced you didn't tell them anything else."

"Then why would they have walked into the constabulary?"

I marched up to the constabulary house and walked in to find Inspector Grimsby seated behind Constable Bell's desk. Since he was so much taller than Bell, he looked as if he was seated behind a toy desk in Bell's raised chair.

"What did you tell them?" he demanded.

"That you were in charge and if they wanted to know anything, to ask you."

"Loose lips sink ships, Mrs. Redmond."

I crossed my arms and stared down at him. "I told them nothing. Did they tell you someone threatened to throw me out of the Women's Institute for not telling them all the juicy details? Who were these women demanding details?"

"The chair, Frances Otterfield, and Lady Lydia Fletcher."

"At least they can't throw you out of the WI, Inspector." But why were these two so determined to find out what had happened? Did they think they knew who did it? Or did they know?

"At least I'm not daft enough to join," the inspector told me.

Chapter Six

"They can certainly destroy a murder investigation, as could you for spreading the details around the village," the inspector continued. "They were determined to find out exactly what we knew. If I didn't know better, those ladies had a reason to kill Mrs. Bryant." Inspector Grimsby ran a hand over his scalp and then quickly lowered his hand.

"What reason would they have, Inspector?"

"I don't know, so you are going to find out."

"Me? But I'm new here."

"So am I, but no one will answer my questions. You, on the other hand, are one of them. You're just a village lady. You can ask all sorts of questions and all they'll think is you're being nosy."

"But—"

"I need your help if I'm ever going to solve this."

I saw the serious expression on his face. "What happened?"

"The ladies in the manor house are threatening to go to the chief constable of the county. It will hurt my career if I'm pulled off the investigation, and then you'll get someone who will choose a killer at random and have them executed just to say they closed the case."

That was the last thing anyone wanted. "Where is Constable Bell?"

"In his quarters."

"Get him out here, and we'll make a start."

Constable Bell came out a few minutes later looking uneasy but curious. "Now, Constable, tell me everything you know about the victim."

He looked at me blankly. "Mrs. Bryant?"

"Yes. Was she born in this village?"

"Yes. Phyllis Castle as she was then. She went to the village school and married a local farmer's son, Herbie Bryant. He died in the influenza outbreak after the Great War and they didn't have any children. She didn't get along with his family when he was alive and after he died, it was worse.

"The only way they could get rid of her was to rent her a cottage in the village and settle some money on her. Then, pleading poverty, she got old Dr. Forrester to take her on as his office help. Only part-time, but it suited her. People thought she wanted to marry the doc, but he was at least smart enough to avoid that. After Dr. Forrester died, his daughter—she lives in Manchester—sold the practice to Dr.

Sampson.

"Dr. Sampson isn't as easygoing as old Doc Forrester, and he and Mrs. Bryant didn't get along. He finally fired her and got someone new this past winter."

"What exactly was the problem between them?"

"I don't know. They had a big falling-out, but I don't know why."

"Put down 'Dr. Sampson, falling out, why?'" I said. Grimsby was already writing.

"Is there any more of her family, the Castles, still in the village or the surrounding area?" Grimsby asked.

"No. She was the last of them."

"What about the Bryants?" I continued.

"There's two left, a brother running the family farm and a sister teaching in Banbury. A couple of the nieces and nephews are working on the farm and a couple others are in factories or the military," Bell said.

"Talk to the brother first, then we'll go to the sister to find out anything we didn't find out from the brother. How much money was she getting from them at her death? Who owns the cottage now?" Grimsby nodded to himself as he wrote. "Or, rather, how long was the rent paid up for?"

"And then there's the rest of the village," I said.

"That's your field," Grimsby said.

"Bell, was she one to start feuds? Hold a grudge? Lay claim to positions of power or possessions that weren't necessarily hers?"

"Oh, aye. She bullied the last secretary of the WI out of her job by claiming she wasn't competent. And then she took over before they could have an election. It was decided it was easier to just elect her, Mrs. Bryant, that is, than argue with her."

"She didn't want to be chair?"

"Too much work. Mrs. Bryant wasn't one for hard work. A little dictation and a lot of gossip was all she was good for."

"Anything malicious, Bell?" Grimsby asked.

"Mostly about the state of people's marriages and who didn't keep a clean house. People ignored her unless they were bent toward gossip themselves."

"Did she get on with Mrs. Hunter? She did take Mrs. Bryant's job," I added.

"It was the doctor she held against," Bell said. "Especially after she found out she couldn't get around Mrs. Hunter. About a week after Mrs. Hunter took over, she came in to work to find Mrs. Bryant rooting through the medical records. Mrs. Hunter has been raising five boys. It took her but a moment to get the records away from Mrs. Bryant and put them back in the file drawers before shoving her out the door. Mrs. Bryant complained to me about being thrown out, but Mrs. Hunter complained to the doctor, who was waiting when we went down to the surgery."

"What did she want in those records?" I asked, seeing a whole extra possibility of motive for murder.

"I never asked whose they were. Dr. Sampson told her

to leave and not come back unless it was as a patient, and otherwise to never set foot in the office again."

"What happened then?" Grimsby asked.

"She snapped at me for not doing my job and slunk off home."

"So, she made an enemy of you by saying you didn't do your job," I said.

"I'm used to it. It's more likely she'd have killed me for not doing her bidding," Bell replied.

"Mrs. Redmond, could you speak to Mrs. Hunter for me? Take Constable Bell with you to make it official, without putting her on her guard for being too official."

"She doesn't go back to work until Monday," I told him. "Dr. Sampson doesn't have regular surgery hours on weekends since he just handles emergencies then. Or do you want us to question her at home?"

"Where do you think she'll be more inclined to talk?"

"Between cooking and cleaning up after five boys, I suspect her weekends are very busy. Let's try her Monday morning at the doctor's surgery. Now, if you want to question Dr. Sampson, I would try him on the weekend, if you can catch him on a quiet day."

Grimsby gave me a reluctant smile. "How early can you and Bell go over to see the doctor tomorrow?"

"I think the doctor would prefer to be questioned by regular police officers," I told him. Bell watched us both carefully, turning his head from side to side as we fired our opinions back and forth.

"I've been ordered back to Oxford for the weekend to give a report to the chief constable. With any luck, I'll be back sometime Sunday. If I need to follow up on your interview, I can do it when I return."

That told me if I was to do any investigating, it had to be now. "I should be ready by nine, Constable. We'll try Dr. Sampson then."

"Who had she been gossiping about lately?" Grimsby asked.

"No one that I'd heard," I said.

"Mr. MacDonald," the constable said. "Her lodger. She felt he was wandering around the village at night too much. Asking too many questions."

Grimsby wrote some notes on his pad. "Now, Constable, tell me about Frances Otterfield," Grimsby said.

Bell, surprised to be called on again, looked at him. "Sir?"

"Frances Otterfield."

"She comes from Oxford, sir, the daughter of a pub owner. She came here when she married Jim Otterfield, the village butcher. She was in her late twenties, he was in his thirties when they wed. No children. Thought of as honest and reputable. No trouble with us or the tax people or the rationing board."

"She works in the shop?" I asked.

"She keeps the books and works the counter part-time.

They have a nephew of Jim's, who is apprenticed to the business."

"A butcher's wife is the perfect chair for the Women's Institute, but I can't picture her as a friend, a social equal, of Lady Lydia Fletcher. You realize the title is earl," I said.

The inspector paled. "She's a countess? That's all I need."

"She was for a year or two. Then her husband was killed in the Battle of Britain, RAF, and the title moved to his younger brother, now also deceased. However, the younger brother had an heir, so the current earl is a five- or six-month-old baby."

"So is she or isn't she a countess, or a dowager countess, or something?" Grimsby looked as confused as I felt by the situation.

"Her mother-in-law is the dowager countess, since she's the baby's grandmother," Bell stated firmly if incorrectly, and I wasn't going to bother to correct him. "That's Lady Agatha. Lady Lydia is the baby's aunt. Lady Jane, who prefers Jane, is the baby's mother.

"And they're all living in the lodge, since the MOD took over the big house," Bell said, finally on solid ground.

"Since 1938 or thereabouts, they've earned themselves three sets of death duties? They must be broke," Grimsby said.

"Yes, so the one thing Lady Lydia can cling to is her title. Then why is she so friendly with a butcher's wife?" I asked.

"I'll go through the records for anything we have on either woman. Do you know their maiden names?" Grimsby asked.

Both Bell and I shook our heads.

"No matter, I should be able to dig that out. Anything else?"

None of us had anything.

"So we have a brother and sister who are probably tired of paying off a disliked sister-in-law, an MOD employee tired of being gossiped about for his nocturnal habits, a doctor who fired Mrs. Bryant over some kind of disagreement, and a constable accused of not doing his job. They all sound as if they're weak reasons for murder." Grimsby shook his head. "We're going to have to dig deeper."

* * *

Constable Bell stopped by Esther's house precisely at nine the next morning. I was ready, a miracle since I'd been up half the night with a teething baby. Stevie, who was fed and changed, was now cooing happily for Nanny Goldie and Becca and chewing on a spoon.

I suppose I should have felt guilty leaving Stevie behind, but I was ready for a situation where I didn't feel so completely incompetent. Teething babies were more difficult to deal with than tightlipped adults.

As we approached the surgery, we could see the doctor's car parked around the side by the door to the house.

At a nod from Bell, I went first around to the side door and rang the buzzer. The doctor, in trousers, slippers, and shirt sleeves, not to mention crutches, answered the door.

"Dr. Sampson, Inspector Grimsby has asked us to clarify a few things with you while he's in Oxford. Would now be convenient?"

"I've been up half the night with a breech birth and I'm tired. You might not get the answers you want."

"If they're truthful, that's what we want. May we come in?"

He stepped back, not an easy thing to do on crutches, and I walked into the drawing room. The two men followed me in. I gestured toward a chair and he nodded.

Once we sat, I asked, "Are the crutches easier to get around on at home than a cane?"

"When I'm on a call, I need to have one arm free for my bag. While I prefer to get around on two crutches and can do it in the house, while tending the sick I can only use one. Why? Is that important?"

"I have no idea," I admitted. "Idle curiosity. Why did you fire Mrs. Bryant as your office secretary?"

Sampson leaned back in his chair and smiled, completely relaxed. "You don't beat around the bush. You've done this before, I imagine."

"I can't answer. Official Secrets Act."

He nodded. "I shouldn't answer you either, but I don't like murder. It's not right."

"We agree on something." I replied with a smile.

"I don't approve of gossip, particularly gossip gathered from my medical records."

"She was going through your patient files and then telling the neighbors what she had read?" I hadn't expected that, but then suddenly it made sense.

"I caught her going through the patient files twice. I warned her and let it go at that since she said she needed the job. And then a patient accused me of telling a third party about details of their medical history. I hadn't. It would be completely unethical."

"It had been Mrs. Bryant?"

"I talked to this 'third party' and found out it was her."

"It was then that you fired her?" This was as if I had to pull the words from him one at a time.

"Yes. I could hardly do otherwise."

"Is there any chance she was blackmailing people with what she'd learned from your files?" Constable Bell asked.

"I've been here less than two years, and in that time, I haven't seen or heard anything worthy of blackmail," Dr. Sampson told him with a shake of his head.

"Whose records did Mrs. Bryant look at, or try to look at?" I asked.

"I didn't pay any attention. It didn't make any difference. Looking at any of them was wrong."

"How long had Mrs. Bryant worked in the office before you came here?" I asked.

"Fifteen years, at least. Perhaps closer to twenty."

"And in all that time, she had access to Dr. Forrester's records." I looked at Constable Bell.

"But if she was blackmailing someone over their old medical records, why would they wait for ten, fifteen, twenty years before they killed her?" Bell asked me. "Doesn't make sense."

"Something changed," I told him.

"I fired her," Dr. Sampson said. "She couldn't get any new victims if she was blackmailing anyone. And I definitely mean if."

"Or maybe something she saw recently reminded her of something in the old files. Something that didn't set off any alarm bells for you, Dr. Sampson, and something related that hadn't set off any alarms for Dr. Forrester many years ago. A suspicious death? Or an accidental poisoning?" I looked from one man to the other. "How many deaths have there been in Chipping Ford in the past two years?"

"Half a dozen or so," Dr. Sampson said. "Nothing suspicious."

"And a few disappearances. But they eventually turn up in the service or working in a factory or on a farm," the constable assured me.

"Doctor, would it be against your medical ethics to give me a list of everyone who has died in and around Chipping Ford since you arrived here, along with their age?"

"You won't find anything."

"Humor me."

The doctor put up his hands. "All right."

"And Constable, please check to make sure all the disappearances in the last two years have been resolved," I told him.

Chapter Seven

Constable Bell left Dr. Sampson's to start going through the records of missing persons while I waited for the doctor to give me a list of everyone who'd died in Chipping Ford and environs in the last two years. He had a book of death certificates and he copied out the information I asked for.

When he handed it over, I said, "I see why you think this will get us nowhere." They had all been above sixty, and half above eighty. "Do any of them stick in your mind?"

"Oddly enough, yes. Most of these patients died in their beds after an illness. But one, Henrietta Johnson, fell from a path halfway into Wenmire Brook and was dead before she was noticed."

"Drowned?"

"No sign of that. She had a puzzling head wound, but since there are all sorts of rocks along the banks of the stream just along where she fell, it was ruled an accident."

"Did anyone benefit?"

"She rented her cottage and the ground around it. She did have some nice furniture and a bit of money put away that was split between a son and two daughters. The older girl was having to take care of her mother and keeping up with her growing family, so her mother's death made her life easier. But hardly a motive," he said.

"Was the older daughter badly overworked?"

"No. But in my office one day, she admitted to finding all the demands on her time overwhelming. I convinced her to talk to her sister about helping out. This might be why I remember, because shortly after that, she and her sister had a very public argument and a day or two later, their mother died."

Dr. Sampson shook his head. "What made it memorable was after their mother's death, the younger daughter told everyone she could that her older sister had killed her mother. Insisted on an inquest, which her mother's death required anyway. Told the coroner she was sure her sister had murdered their mother because she was too lazy to take proper care of her."

"That would only give us a motive for killing Mrs. Bryant if Mrs. Bryant tried to blackmail the older daughter over her mother's death and she really had killed her mother." That would require we prove two murders.

"I doubt that. The daughter wasn't the type to kill anyone. And certainly not her mother."

"And if it weren't true, she'd never have submitted to

blackmail." I studied the doctor. "This woman isn't overly concerned with the opinions of her neighbors, is she?"

"No. She doesn't run a shop in the village or anything along those lines."

"What did the inquest find?" I thought that would be very important if Mrs. Bryant wanted to blackmail anyone.

"Accidental death, most likely from a fall in poor light and with an underlying heart condition."

"All right. We'll put her to one side as a possibility for Inspector Grimsby. What is the daughter's name?"

"Patricia Sharp. But really, you can't believe…"

"No. Just so we can give complete records to Inspector Grimsby."

"Why exactly did Grimsby go back to Oxford?" Dr. Sampson asked.

"To look into the background of a couple of people who have acted strangely. Strangely enough that if they weren't involved in the murder, he believes they must have a strong suspicion of who the killer is."

"I hope this isn't going to involve my medical records."

"No." I tried to reassure him. "If it involves anyone's, it would be Dr. Forrester's."

"I can't allow you to go reading all my files in the hopes of finding something incriminating."

"If, and this is a big if, we have to look at an old medical file, it will be to find out something specific about a specific person."

Dr. Sampson studied me for a minute. "I don't think you are enjoying this."

"The thought that a neighbor was driven to murder by another neighbor who was a gossip or even a blackmailer?" I shook my head. "No, there is nothing to enjoy."

I started walking back to Esther's house when Mr. MacDonald caught up with me. "They've found me a new billet in the village," he told me.

"That's good. Who?"

"Mrs. Coffey. Her daughter married a farmer, so we'll eat well." He smiled and patted his stomach. "Mrs. Bryant wasn't a good, or a generous, cook."

"I think Jane mentioned Mrs. Coffey cooks for the family at the lodge and the food is good," I told him.

"Another sign that we'll be eating well."

"You want to stay in Chipping Ford with a murderer in the village?" I asked.

"As I don't know enough to blackmail anybody, I'm not worried." After a moment, Mr. MacDonald wiped the smile from his face. "I'm sorry. It's not a subject to joke about."

"No, it's not," I said in a stuffy tone. "But Inspector Grimsby seems as if he's a thorough policeman, so I think he'll find the killer."

"Grimsby, eh?"

"Do you know him?" And why, I added to myself.

"He's a contact for my office. Afraid I can't say any more."

"Of course. Official Secrets Act."

"Yes. Grimsby. What a surprise. He's a good policeman," Mr. MacDonald said and then waved goodbye as I reached my garden gate.

* * *

The rest of the day saw us out in the garden until we were forced inside by a rainy afternoon. I sat Stevie on my lap and he laughed as he watched the antics of Johnny and Becca. I was warned by Esther that he was taking notes for when he became a little older.

Mercifully, he was up watching the older two children enough that day that he was tired out at bedtime and slept better than he had the last few days. Then for breakfast Sunday morning, Nanny Goldie made him a little watery gruel and he loved it, chewing on the spoon with his gums and eating maybe half the cereal that went into his mouth. The other half was wiped off his chin.

We dressed up and walked the short distance to church, where Johnny and Becca stayed in the church creche and Stevie spent his time being held in my arms. He grew fussy during the sermon, and as I didn't think I would be missing anything, I slipped out onto the porch. A minute later, Jane arrived with Andrew.

This was Stevie's first time to really notice Andrew, and he was fascinated by a baby close to him in age. Jane and I sat next to each other on a bench in the porch with the boys on our laps as they kicked their feet and swung their arms and cooed.

"I think Andrew has grown since I last saw him," I said.

"Stevie definitely has."

We talked about the babies for a minute, and then Jane said, "Has Lydia forced that Inspector Grimsby off the investigation? She was trying to."

"Why would she do that?"

"I don't know. She wants him replaced by someone she can order around. Someone who won't try too hard to find Mrs. Bryant's killer."

"Why would Lydia, who lives in this village, want to allow a killer to go free and maybe kill another neighbor? Or herself?"

"I don't know, but I know Lydia isn't protecting herself. The four of us—Agatha, Lydia, Andrew, and I—were together at the lodge." She shrugged. "Fixing the gutter by the back door where it pours in every time it rains."

I tried to picture that. "Even Agatha?"

"She held Andrew so he could watch me. He doesn't care to be separated from me. If she'd moved away, he would have screamed."

"And Lydia?"

"I went up the ladder and she stood on the ground and handed me things so I could clear the blockage. We wanted to get it done before it was full dark. And then we went into the kitchen and ate potatoes and cheese for dinner. It was Mrs. Coffey's night off."

I couldn't help teasing her. "My, you do live a glamorous life, don't you, Lady Jane Fletcher."

"Don't I?" She returned my grin. "But you see, none of us could have done it. So whatever her reason, and I think it's just snobbishness, it wasn't her."

"It wasn't any of us either, provable by Stevie. He was teething and he had a cold. We had to call Dr. Sampson. I was walking the floor with him while Magda and Nanny Goldie and Esther were trying to build a tent for steam and rubbing his gums. Even more of a circus than fixing your roof," I ended with a smile.

"So that only means the rest of the village," Jane said. "But how do we keep her from pulling Inspector Grimsby from the case?"

"I don't know, but he went back to Oxford Friday to look into a couple of possibilities. I hope he talked to the chief constable while he was there. We both know Constable Bell can't handle this on his own, and Grimsby seems to be thorough."

"Lydia is used to bossing Bell around. And he's used to being bossed around by her."

"How long have you been spending time in this village?" I asked as the strains of the last hymn leaked out of the door.

"Only since Peter and I started dating, and that was mostly in London just at the start of the war. The first time I came here was for our wedding, in this church, in the early days of 1940."

"Was Dr. Forrester still here then?"

"No, he had already died, and his daughter was trying to sell the practice. She had a couple of arguments with Mrs. Bryant. Loud ones."

"Do you know what they were about?" I asked, but at that moment, the congregation started pouring out of the double doors from the sanctuary.

I knew Esther had to collect Johnny and Becca from the creche and that would take some time, but Lady Agatha was almost the first one out, closely followed by Lady Lydia. Jane had already gathered up her things and straightened Andrew's pram, so she was ready to leave.

"Mrs. Redmond," Lady Agatha said, "how is your baby doing?"

"Teething. I'm sure you remember that stage."

She laughed a short, socially adept sound. "Yes. Still gives me nightmares. Good day."

"Good day." I watched Jane follow the other two ladies up the path to the right, wishing she'd had time to tell me what the arguments were about.

Esther came out last with some of the creche mothers and their children. "Ready to come home?"

"Yes, and looking forward to lunch."

"So are we all," a friend of Esther's said. I had met her once or twice before. She had two little boys who seemed capable of stopping a German invasion by themselves. Or leveling the village on their own. At the moment, they were laying siege to each other and threatening to trip any unsuspecting parishioners coming out of the church.

We headed home, where Magda had fixed us what felt as if it were a feast. Root vegetables soup with a pork broth, cheesy biscuits, and a sweet pudding. We enjoyed it, Stevie drinking some of the broth, and then I fed him before we heard from Constable Bell.

I followed him back to the police constabulary, where I found I was glad to discover Inspector Grimsby had returned. "The chief constable was pleased we were finding various suspects. He's letting me run with it for another week."

"Where do we stand with our suspects?" I asked.

"Tell me what you learned first," Grimsby said.

I couldn't argue. He was the officer in charge. "Dr. Sampson caught Mrs. Bryant going through medical files twice, so he fired her and they argued. Not long after he hired Mrs. Hunter, she caught Mrs. Bryant again going through medical files. Those two ladies argued and Mrs. Hunter threw her out. I thought it was for blackmail, but Dr. Sampson doesn't think there's anything there to blackmail anyone with."

"Anything else?"

"She bullied the former WI secretary out of her position and took it over."

"That won't do any good, Mrs. Redmond," Bell said. "I know the lady. She died three years ago."

"We can eliminate her," I said with a shrug. "Mrs. Bryant also fought with Dr. Forrester's daughter, so you might want to check with her to find out what that was about and whether she had an alibi."

"What about you, Bell?" Grimsby asked.

"The only person who saw anything was Mrs. Withins."

"The friend of Lady Agatha from the WI meeting?" I asked.

"Yes. Mrs. Withins is a wealthy widow. Her husband was a lawyer in Oxford. He left her that big house on the other side of the village." Bell flipped over a page in his notebook. "She was letting her cat in about half seven by the back door when she saw a woman entering Mrs. Bryant's back door."

"Could she recognize her?"

"No. She was too far away and Mrs. Bryant's back door was in shadow. Her back door faces the side of Mrs. Bryant's cottage, so she sees everyone in silhouette."

"Then how does she know—?"

"She was wearing a dress." Bell looked through a couple of pages of notes. "Or a suit. Definitely a skirt."

"Anyone in the area wear a kilt, Constable?" Grimsby asked.

"No, sir." Bell saw us exchange a smile. "Oh, it's a joke. No, sir. Not a kilt. Probably a skirt."

"The pathologist says the knife strike could easily have been done by a woman," Grimsby told us.

"Learn anything else about the case, sir?" I said.

Grimsby pulled out his battered notebook and said, "First, Lady Lydia. Maiden name is Gordon."

"You mean the same as the MP for Oxford? Any relation?"

"Yes. Her father was against the marriage due to some rumor about Matthew Fletcher's background."

"He wasn't very old. Was it about something he did while he was in Oxford?" I asked.

"The only thing I heard was 'He's gone now, it doesn't matter to Lydia and they had no children, so there's no point in raking up all that ancient history now.' And this from the only person I could find who knew not only Matthew Fletcher, but also Winthrop Gordon, Lydia's father."

"All right, let's park that to one side. What about Frances Otterfield?"

"Her parents ran a pub. Her father was tight with coins, her mother was socially ambitious. There was a major falling-out when Frances was sixteen or seventeen involving an Oxford student. They had been going out, sneaking out, really, and then one night there was some kind of accident. Her father didn't want to pay to have a doctor look her over and by the time her mother finally forced him to, Frances nearly died."

Grimsby continued. "The boy was sent down and she never saw him again. She met Jim Otterfield a few years later while working in her parents' pub and they later married and moved to Chipping Ford."

"It would be easy enough to see the details of that in Dr. Forrester's medical notes and could easily be found and understood by Mrs. Bryant. But it hardly sounds as if it's gossip material. Or blackmail material," I said.

"I learned more. I spoke to Phyllis Bryant's brother-in-law and sister-in-law," Grimsby said. "They both admitted Mrs. Bryant wanted them to up her allowance and they refused, but they both have good alibis for the time of the murder. It wasn't them."

Somebody with a good reason to want her dead had to be available that night.

Chapter Eight

"So, we now have three not very likely suspects—Dr. Sampson, Mrs. Otterfield, and Lady Lydia Fletcher. Any other possibilities, Mrs. Redmond?" Inspector Grimsby sounded equal parts disgusted and annoyed.

"First off, Dr. Sampson and Lady Lydia have good alibis. I had Dr. Sampson make me a list of all the deaths in Chipping Ford since he arrived here," Constable Bell said. "There was only one, Henrietta Johnson, that looked odd to him. Died of a head wound walking along a stream bank. She didn't drown. It was early and probably dark out. She could have tripped, collapsed from a heart attack or stroke, anything, and hit her head on a rock. There's plenty of them along that part of the Wenmire."

Inspector Grimsby looked from Bell to me. "Or someone picked up a rock and hit her, killing her. Was anyone suspected?"

"Her older daughter had been taking care of her and

was getting tired of doing all the work alone. Dr. Sampson suggested she get her younger sister to help. Two days after they had a very public row, Mrs. Johnson was found dead."

"Has anyone investigated this?" Grimsby asked Bell.

"The coroner ruled the death accidental," Bell replied.

"Where were the sisters?"

"The older sister was suspected since she was tired of having to take care of everything for her mother, but she was part of a delegation speaking to a committee in London on the role of older people in the war effort," Bell said. "She traveled with two other women who knew her and verified that she was with them on the early train, getting in to London about the same time her mother was dying on the path."

"And the younger sister?"

"Doing the morning chores around the house, fixing breakfast for her two children before going to her employment in an office in the manor house here. It's been taken over by the MOD," Bell added.

"She could still have done it," Grimsby said. "If she didn't have a great deal to do or a great distance to do it."

"How old are her children?" I asked.

"The boy is eighteen and out of school. Has a dodgy ticker and he couldn't serve, so he's working in a town clerk's office in Oxford. The girl is thirteen and is in school on track to take at least her O levels." Bell once again showed his knowledge of the village and everyone in it.

"And this woman couldn't be bothered helping to take care of her mother?" Grimsby asked, still sounding annoyed. At least now he wasn't annoyed with me.

"Apparently not," Bell replied. "Peggy Norris was the younger by several years and spoiled by the rest of the family when she was young. She's always had an attitude that she's a bit better than the rest of us."

"It doesn't matter who took care of their mother," Grimsby said with a sigh. "We're interested in who killed Mrs. Bryant, and there's no connection between Mrs. Bryant and Mrs. Johnson, is there?"

Bell shook his head.

"Mrs. Bryant didn't try to start rumors about either of Mrs. Johnson's daughters from Dr. Sampson's records, did she? As far as we know?" I asked.

"Sounds as if she had no grounds to," Grimsby said. "Just another dead end."

"Could she have tried to blackmail a shopkeeper or someone over a large rationing fraud? Some blackmail that has nothing to do with Dr. Sampson or medical records?" I asked.

"Possible. Makes a good motive for murder. Have you heard anything about that, Bell?"

"I haven't heard of anyone in Chipping Ford fiddling with the rationing records. We're a pretty law-abiding group in this village. Children chucking stones and too much noise from the pub on Saturday night is about as exciting as it gets around here."

"Until someone gets murdered," I reminded him. He shuddered in reply.

"I want you two to talk to Mrs. Hunter at the doctor's surgery office tomorrow morning. Find out about all of her dealings with Mrs. Bryant and her alibi," Grimsby said. "Meanwhile, does anyone know where Mrs. Bryant did her banking?"

"At the post office in the grocer's here in the village."

"So, we need to find her bank book. Bell, come on, we're going on a hunt in her cottage."

"Nine tomorrow morning, Constable?" I asked as I headed for the door.

Bell nodded, his attention already on Grimsby.

* * *

The next morning, I was ready and waiting for Bell when he arrived on Esther's doorstep. I told Esther I was leaving, but she was busy playing with Stevie and only heard me with half her attention.

We walked over to the doctor's surgery. When we entered, we were the only ones in the waiting room. I told Mrs. Hunter that we were there at Inspector Grimsby's request to find out about every interaction she had had with Mrs. Bryant.

"Whatever for?" she asked.

"The only thing we can find that Mrs. Bryant did that was out of the ordinary was trying to get into those records."

I gestured at the file cabinets along the far wall.

She considered for a moment and then said, "Come into the office." She opened the door for us and shut it behind us. Then she nodded to two chairs off to the side where we could sit and not be seen by any patients who might come in.

"Tell me what occurred between you two in this office," I said.

"Which time?"

Bell looked surprised but I hid mine. "Let's start with the first time."

"It was about my third day in the office. Dr. Sampson had warned me not to let her near the patient files. She walked back here as if it were her home and started rummaging through those files." She gestured toward a couple of old file cabinets in a corner of the office.

"And then?"

"I stopped what I was doing, walked over to her and told her to leave. She told me she'd only be a minute, she'd left something here. I told her too bad and treated her to a shifting the same as my boys get when they're into something they shouldn't be."

"Did she have anything in her hands?"

"Not when I finished with her. I turned her around and marched her out of the office, shutting and locking the door behind her. She told me I hadn't heard the last of this and she stomped off."

I looked at Mrs. Hunter's hands. They were large and rough skinned from caring for five lively boys. She looked capable of marching Mrs. Bryant out of any office. "Which drawer in those file cabinets? Do you remember?"

"Third down on the left and the second on the right."

"All right, now how about the next time?"

"There was only one other time, about a week later. Surgery had closed for the day, the doctor had popped over to his house to get something for his rounds, and I was cleaning up the surgery and not able to see the office when I heard something. I leaned back and saw Mrs. Bryant going into the office. I knew it wasn't allowed, so I dropped what I was doing and rushed over here."

"What was she looking for this time?"

"The same as before. She was pulling files out of the third drawer down in the left-hand cabinet."

"And?"

"I stopped her, didn't I? I pulled those files out of her hands and slammed them down on top of the file cabinet and told her to leave. We were arguing when Dr. Sampson returned and immediately told her to leave empty-handed. She let him know she wouldn't let it end there. 'There are scandals aplenty in these files. And scandals find a way out into the light of day. Don't you forget that,' she said."

For a moment with those words, Mrs. Bryant came alive again.

"Which doctor wrote up those files she was going for?

Dr. Forrester or Sampson?"

"Forrester."

"Do you know what years they were from?" I hoped having a date for the files would lead to some village event that people remembered.

She shrugged. "Any time from before the Great War to 1938."

"What's different about those files than the ones along here?" I pointed to the rest of the cabinets.

"Dr. Sampson hasn't had reason to refer to the files in those two cabinets since he arrived here."

"Because the patients are dead?" I asked.

"Moved away, dead, have nothing to do with the patient's health now. There must be other reasons why Dr. Sampson hasn't had reason to refer to them, but I don't know why, do I?" Mrs. Hunter looked at me as if I weren't as quick as her sons.

"Do you remember whose files Mrs. Bryant pulled out of the drawers either time?"

"No."

"Not a single name?"

"No. I was too busy pulling them away from her. Dr. Sampson put them away while I threw her out of the office."

"Do you think he'd let us look at the files in those two drawers to see why they were so important to Mrs. Bryant?"

"No, and I hope he doesn't. She was a vicious, vain old witch without a good word for anyone."

"Where were you on the night Mrs. Bryant was murdered?"

"Home, cooking, cleaning, dealing with my boys."

We heard the outside door open.

"You'd better go. We'll be busy with the living," she told us and rose to open the door and let us out into the waiting room.

We thanked her and went on our way.

Once we were outside and out of hearing distance from anyone, I asked Constable Bell, "What did you find out from the search for Mrs. Bryant's bank book?"

"She had four regular deposits each month. One was from her husband's family. They admit it. The other three were small and in cash. She put them in, so we don't know who they were from and no one has volunteered the information."

"Do you think all three were blackmail payments?"

Bell nodded.

"She wasn't doing part-time work for anyone in the village? Childminding or mending or anything?"

"No." Constable Bell shook his head. "I keep forgetting you didn't know her. She had no interest in work. She had a lot of interest in money, but none in any way you could legally obtain it."

"It didn't appear to be the cottage of someone who had a great deal of money," I told him.

"You didn't look through her cabinets and wardrobes,"

Bell said, lowering his voice so much I had a hard time hearing him. "Silk underclothes. Real silk. Prewar material. Biscuits. Expensive brands of biscuits in their original unopened tins. Tins of exotic teas. Top-brand face cream. Oh, no, she had expensive tastes, if you looked inside her dressing table or wardrobe."

Mrs. Bryant had had an extra source of income until she was fired by Dr. Sampson. "Were these three payments a month new since she was let go by the doctor? As a replacement, perhaps."

"No. Two of them had been going on for at least ten years. The third one began just a month before she was fired."

"How odd. If someone was paying blackmail, or anything, for ten years, why would they suddenly kill Mrs. Bryant?" What Constable Bell was telling me made no sense.

"Maybe she was raising her rates since she'd lost her job and her victim couldn't afford it anymore." Bell shrugged. "Let's go back to the constabulary and talk to the inspector."

We walked up the hill to the constabulary house and Bell filled the inspector in on what we'd learned from Mrs. Hunter.

"Then the files we want, that would point to the blackmail victims who could be the killer, are in those two drawers of old files from Dr. Forrester," Inspector Grimsby said.

"Yes."

"Let's go talk to Dr. Sampson." He straightened his long narrow body up from the small desk and headed out of the constabulary, Bell behind him.

That was when I saw the bank book on the desk. "I'll wait here for you, in case you need me for something."

Bell shut the door, and I was alone with the bank book. I waited a moment, and when they didn't return, I sat behind the desk and began to read the bank book backward.

There were four payments into the account in the past month, all spread out throughout the month. The month before, three of the payments were the same amount and one was smaller. The month before that, there were two the same amount as the month after and two smaller than the month after.

The month before that, there were more payments, which must have marked the end of Mrs. Bryant's employment with Dr. Sampson. All three of the smaller payments were smaller than they had been in the final month in her bank book.

If these smaller payments were blackmail, this marked a change. A change that could have marked the threat that ended her life.

I turned back to the beginning, which said this was the second bank book, continuing, for Phyllis Bryant. In the first month, all the payments were smaller, but we had been in an economic depression where her in-laws would have had little cash to pay her. Dr. Forrester's patients would have been less likely to be able to pay him his going rate, and so Mrs. Bryant's weekly pay would have been less than it would have been lately, now that everyone was holding down well-paying jobs for the Ministry of Defense.

The two small payments were in cash, and both were smaller than the size of the payments currently showing up in the bank book.

I turned to the back again. There I found the first of the third stream of payments had begun two months prior to Mrs. Bryant's termination from employment. But what was she blackmailing anyone for?

Something had happened the previous autumn in Chipping Ford that someone was willing to pay Mrs. Bryant to keep quiet about. Something only Mrs. Bryant knew about, or there wouldn't be any point in paying her. And I suspected whatever this thing was that someone had done, it was illegal.

Without seeing those medical records, I couldn't possibly guess at the exact crime. I hoped Inspector Grimsby would need my help and would eventually tell me.

Chapter Nine

There was nothing else I could do, so I went home, hoping the police would come looking for me to give them assistance.

I didn't think Inspector Grimsby would. He seemed very capable. But now that I was involved, and I was living in this village with my infant son where we now had a killer on the loose, I wanted to help. I wanted the killer stopped.

It wasn't until close to blackout time that we had a knock on the front door. It was Constable Bell, telling us one of the upstairs curtains had been pushed aside, probably by a youngster. Esther thanked him and headed upstairs while I asked him in a whisper, "Did you see Dr. Forrester's medical records?"

"No. Dr. Sampson doesn't want to turn them over. Doesn't feel he has the right."

"Is there anything we can do?" I asked with hope in my voice.

"No." He made a glum face.

"If I hear anything about anyone being blackmailed, I'll let you know." I gave him a small smile.

"I'm not completely certain about people here in Chipping Ford being blackmailed by Mrs. Bryant," Bell said. "I mean, people around here?"

"How else would you explain her bank book?"

"You shouldn't have looked at that." The constable looked furious.

"Well, I did. And to me it appears to be blackmail payments. What else could it be?"

"The inspector thinks it could be several different things."

"What?" I tried to sound merely curious, but there was belligerence in my tone that I couldn't control.

"Ask the inspector." The constable glared back at me.

I gave up. "What's more, this newest victim, Constable, I think has broken the law. Something you don't know about yet."

"The inspector doesn't think anyone has been blackmailed."

"What do you think, Constable?" I held his gaze.

"I think we need proof." He returned my stare and headed out into the dark.

I shut the door behind him.

"What were you and Constable Bell talking about?" Esther asked when I came into the drawing room.

"I've seen Mrs. Bryant's bank book," I told her. "It was sitting out in the police constabulary and I had a chance, so I looked through it. She was getting the same three small amounts of cash every month. One started last autumn, and the other two go back more than ten years."

"Her pay from working for Dr. Forrester? Money from her husband's family?"

"Her weekly pay and the money from the family were larger and easy to tell where they came from."

"She didn't do any piece work for anyone," Esther said.

"And it wouldn't be the exact same amount every time if it had been," I added.

"How would she learn anything about anyone that she could blackmail them about?"

"She worked in a doctor's surgery. Medical records."

"She was nosy," Esther said, shaking her head, "but we won't figure it out tonight. Now, does Stevie have any clean outgrown clothing? The Mothers' Union is having a clothing swap Wednesday morning. The number of items you bring in that you can swap, you can get that many in a larger size for your child. And best of all, you don't need to use any clothing coupons."

"He's outgrown practically everything. Tomorrow will need to be laundry day."

* * *

All day the next day, Esther, Nanny Goldie, and I spent cleaning and mending and folding children's clothing. It was raining, so Johnny and Becca watched us as they played with their toys. Stevie watched us from his pram, which I'd set beside me.

The kitchen, dining room, and scullery were full of clothes lines and we ran the stove and the fires and the boiler to give off heat to dry everything before the next morning. It felt as if the entire house were steamy and damp.

Esther finished drying Johnny's outgrown clothes at about midnight. I didn't get done until three in the morning, but that included a late-night feeding. Stevie looked adorable, sleeping in his cot, when I finally climbed into bed.

The hall used for the WI meeting was now set up with long rows of tables holding clothes eligible for swap in size order and divided into boys' and girls'. At the end of the table with the infant clothes, there was as much where gender didn't matter and they were all stacked up together.

There was a separate section with children's leather shoes, the two halves looped around each other and sorted by size. I heard Esther lamenting that shoes were harder to find than clothes and more difficult to fit on growing feet.

Most of the mothers had brought their children so they could see how things would fit when held up against their backs or put on their feet. The children, already bored, were starting to run around, shouting and laughing, only to be corralled by teachers, grandmothers, and childless members of the WI.

I pushed Stevie over to where Jane was standing. "Do

you think he's ready for Andrew's outgrown clothes?" I asked.

"Probably, and Stevie's the only one they can go to," she told me.

"It's Stevie's lucky day, then," I said as the president of the Mothers' Union gaveled for silence and then repeated the rules. We each knew how many items we could choose—it was in the Mother's Union book in case of misunderstandings—and we should treat all the clothing carefully and refold everything we unfolded. Then she told us we could begin.

Things were orderly in infants and toddlers, but in the section for five- and six-year-olds, especially boys, chaos reigned. The mothers of the young boys and the teachers alone couldn't manage what would surely turn into a riot. After taking care of their own children, several mothers of teenagers as well as grandmothers dove into the confusion in an effort to keep order in that one small area.

I glanced over to see one little boy by the shoe table pelt another with a pair of brown lace-ups, followed by the open hand of a middle-aged woman across his bottom. I realized that was the son of Esther's friend who had the two boys who seemed equal to bringing down the Third Reich by themselves.

I picked up a shirt and overall combination in blue and found it was a perfect size for Stevie. "That matches his eyes."

"It does," Jane said, looking over from a shirt and short pants outfit. "He has beautiful eyes."

"Is Andrew…? Yes, he has a gorgeous shade of blue eyes, too."

"Yes, he got them from his father. Or maybe my father. Mine are muddy brown," Jane said.

"Mine are sort of purplish rather than blue, but Adam has bright blue eyes," I told her.

"Hold this up to Stevie. I think it will fit him," Jane said, gesturing to a onesie set.

"I guess this gets easier when half their clothing needs to be their school uniform," I said, "and the other half play clothes."

"I hope by the time these two start school, that the war, rationing, and clothing coupons are all a thing of the past," Jane said.

Amen.

At that point, a long dispute started on whether a top and bottom set counted as one or two. It turned out the women counting out the clothing to be given credit for hadn't been consistent, and now there was no way to be completely fair.

It was decided to count each item, top or bottom, as one piece since there was no way to make it right for everyone, which led to much grumbling.

"There's always a problem with something. Last time the little boys were so rowdy that they considered banning them, but the mothers were upset since they wouldn't be able to measure the clothes against their children," Jane told me.

I saw Nanny Goldie taking Johnny out while carrying a stack of rugged-looking clothing. Esther would now be able to focus on finding some clothes for Becca, who I suspected would complain that now all the pretty dresses were picked over. She had no reason to worry. Her grandfather, Sir Henry, would be able to find her a couple of lovely gowns in the middle of Armageddon.

I checked out just after Jane and went out into the sunshine with her to wait for Esther. While we waited, Lady Agatha came out of the church with Mrs. Brown-Dunn and Mrs. Withins and headed in our direction.

"Here comes the coven," Jane murmured with a smile.

When they reached us, Lady Agatha stopped just as Esther came out of the town hall. "I hope you ladies will come by for tea Friday at four o'clock. No children, I'm afraid," Lady Agatha said.

I looked at Esther for how to respond. "We'd love to," she said.

"Yes, that sounds nice." Nice? Where had I parked my brain when I came to Chipping Ford? One of my few skills as a reporter was finding the exact correct word for anything and everything. No wonder my efforts at writing columns for Sir Henry on new motherhood in the countryside were so deplorable.

"Good. We'll see you then. Come along, Jane," Lady Agatha said as she walked away.

Jane gave me a smile and walked off, pushing Andrew in his pram overstuffed with clothes that would fit him through the warmer months.

I couldn't complain. Stevie was well outfitted, too. We walked home and after I put away his new clothes and fed him, I joined everyone for lunch. Stevie napped in his pram. Magda had once again fixed us a delicious lunch using the herbs she grew in her protected herb garden and a little chicken broth.

While Stevie continued to nap, I did some weeding in the vegetable patch. That soon bored me and I went inside to write Sir Henry a letter about the murder in Chipping Ford and my theory about blackmail. A theory at least partially shared by the local police.

I wondered what Sir Henry would make of the murder in our village and my theory about the cause.

That letter, which I mailed while walking Stevie before dinner, came back to my mind after dinner when Constable Bell stopped by and asked me to go to the constabulary house. I put on my hat and coat, asked Esther to keep an eye on my sleeping baby, and walked up the hill.

When I opened the door, I found Inspector Grimsby at Bell's desk, still looking as if he'd been squeezed in to fit. His torso loomed over the writing surface. "I'm afraid I'll be leaving here tomorrow without getting any further on the murder. We'll be carrying out the continuing investigation from Oxford."

"That can't be to make the process more efficient," I told him.

He rose then, straightening to his full height. "No. But there's a black-market ring busy in Oxford, and we need to stop them. Most of the police force has been called up for military service, so resources are stretched miserably thin."

"And catching a black-market ring is more important than catching a killer?" I asked him, annoyance slipping into my tone.

Grimsby stood at attention. "That is the view of my superiors."

"Which is what tells me they aren't superior to you. Not in policing."

He relaxed just a little. "Of course, Constable Bell is free to continue the investigation, calling on anyone he thinks might be of help."

"And if he finds some clues as to who was being blackmailed?"

"Bell should call the Oxford headquarters immediately if he finds any solid evidence of blackmail."

"Bell should?" I raised my eyebrows.

"If you want a response, Bell needs to call. It is my superiors who will allocate any resources. They believe in the chain of command."

"Thank you for your honesty." I paused, needing to say

more. "And thank you for your efforts to find out who killed Mrs. Bryant."

"I'm sorry we couldn't get a faster resolution."

I held out my hand. "Good luck, Inspector Grimsby."

He shook it. "Good luck, Mrs. Redmond."

* * *

The next morning, I found out that everyone in the village knew the inspector had returned to Oxford within a half hour of his leaving. The word arrived through one of the mothers walking Johnny along with some other children to junior school. Magda heard as she stood in line at the grocer's. And I was told by a neighbor as I pushed Stevie's pram down the street.

"Will the village return to normal now?" I asked Esther. I hadn't been there long enough to recognize normal, but I hoped the answer was yes.

"Eventually, maybe. If the police had arrested someone, then we would have gone back to normal within days."

"Because everyone would have felt safe? Instead, we're left with a murderer on the loose and the police can't spend more than a couple of days on solving the crime." I bounced my fists against air in frustration.

"Yes. Which is why you and Constable Bell need to find the killer," Esther said.

"Me?"

"You're trained, Liv. At least as experienced as Constable Bell. Maybe more so. The two of you are the only ones who are."

"What about Stevie?" He was my number one consideration.

"You'll be right here with him. And if you have to pop out for a few minutes, Nanny Goldie or I can watch him." Esther looked at me levelly. "You and Bell have to do this. For the village."

I nodded. I agreed with her in principle. The problem was, without the doctor's records, I had no idea how to proceed.

I spent that day and the next, whether I was feeding Stevie or doing chores, going through everything I'd seen or heard. I certainly had no idea how to clarify anything. Did Grimsby's "superiors" know we were out of our depths? Worse, did they realize what living with a murderer did to an otherwise quiet village?

Any time I was out of doors with Stevie, any time a delivery vehicle drove down the lane, lace curtains twitched. No one spoke to their neighbors in line at the post office for fear they would be thought by the killer to be talking about them.

Esther had to call my name three times to get my attention when it was time to visit Lady Agatha. I put on a woolen skirt and a twinset while Esther wore a sweater dress. We both put on coats, hats, and gloves and hurried up the street to the lodge.

Jane opened the door and welcomed us into the dark-paneled, high-ceilinged front hall. Lydia hovered, gesturing us into what I guessed was the main drawing room. On the other side was a magnificent wide staircase with an ornate railing.

I stood in the hall and looked around. "Wow. And this is only the lodge?"

"I'm afraid so," Lydia said. "Built in the Victorian period, while the main house is Georgian. This was built to house one, the dowager countess, while the main house was designed to house the earl and his entire family."

Lady Agatha—I had come to think of her that way already—rose when we came in and welcomed us with a sweep of her arm that indicated the stuffed chairs where we could sit.

The main feature of the hall and the drawing room was that the walls were all paneled and every inch of them seemed to be covered with oil paintings. I could tell they varied in age and all were painted with talent. Esther recognized the styles of individual artists. She wandered around the room, enraptured.

Several glass-fronted cabinets took up a large part of the hall, giving it the feel of a museum. And every cabinet contained several very large Victorian-looking pieces in china or silver, many of them appearing to be animals or birds. I wandered from one end of the area to the other, finally gazing at a last case, this one full to bursting with miniature silver or china pieces. Two identical christening cups sat next to each other on a low shelf. I bent and saw one was labeled "Matthew 10-4-16" and the other "Peter 17-9-17."

A display of a sword in a glass cabinet on the mantelpiece in the drawing room caught my attention. A small tarnished plaque on the faded velvet lining held the date 20 July 1915. "Was that the date your husband was commissioned?" I asked Lady Agatha.

"Yes. It was a very short war for him, as he was seriously wounded and returned to England not long after. His war was over. If fate hadn't intervened so dramatically, I never would have met him or married him when I did," Lady Agatha said.

"It's nice that something good came out of that war," I said, inwardly cringing as I again said "nice."

I glanced up and then stopped to stare at the large canvas that hung over the fireplace. I recognized Lady Agatha from twenty years before. "Is that you and your husband? And your sons as boys?"

"Happier times."

Lady Agatha and her husband were both painted with blue eyes. So why did one boy have blue eyes and the other grayish ones? Why was her husband painted in his dress military uniform? Lady Agatha's dress and hair told me this had been painted in the 1920s.

I decided there was too much stuff on display in this house to come to any conclusions. I was certain, however, that I wanted to come back and search through all the displays in the hopes I'd find a clue to the murder and how it might be linked to the ladies in the lodge.

Chapter Ten

"It's a—" and then Esther mentioned a painter I had heard of as she came up behind me.

"Yes," Lady Agatha said.

"And you have a Vermeer, a Manet, a Renoir—"

"Two Renoirs, actually."

"When the MOD took over the manor house, we removed all the paintings and silver of any worth," Lady Lydia said, "and brought it here."

"And the most valuable of the furniture and tapestries," Lady Agatha added.

"We had the rest of the furniture, sculptures, and paintings moved to the attic in the manor house," Lydia continued.

The lodge seemed to be a perfect target for blackmailers. And robbers. "Fortunately, your home doesn't seem overcrowded," I said aloud.

"We have a great deal tucked away in the attic. Of

course, we'll need to start selling some of it soon to pay for the death duties." Agatha looked sad at the thought.

"No, we mustn't. This is the Fletcher family heritage. We must save it for Andrew," Lydia said.

"And then the interest piles up until everything will have to go. The manor, the estate, this house, and everything in it," Jane said, glaring at her sister-in-law. "And that's not fair to Andrew or any of us."

"Ladies, please. Our guests don't want to hear about our problems," Agatha said, sounding every inch a lady from another era. "Please take a seat and we'll have tea before it grows cold."

"It's a problem more and more landed families are having, though, isn't it?" I asked, sitting down. "With this terrible war going on and bombs falling and the government short of cash."

"At least the MOD is putting the manor and the estate to good use and paying us well for their presence. Which we are turning around and giving back to the government as payment toward our death duties," Jane said, sounding defeated.

"Of course, not being used to life in the landed aristocracy, all these things don't mean as much to you," Lydia said, without specifying who she meant. She stared at Jane, however, until Jane looked up and saw where her gaze fell. Jane stared back angrily.

"How is your family making out, Lady Lydia?" I asked

quickly to avoid an argument.

"About the same as everyone else. My brother was killed and my father is in poor health. We'll soon have death duties on that estate as well, but it won't be our problem. A cousin will inherit, I believe." Lydia shook her head. "Let's talk about something pleasant."

"Or we could talk about the murder," Esther said cheerfully, taking a sip of tea.

"Do they know who did it yet?" Jane asked, leaning forward in her seat with her cup and saucer.

"No, but I think Mrs. Bryant was a blackmailer," I told her, watching Lady Agatha out of the corner of my eye. I thought she turned pale for a moment, but that could have been my imagination.

"No wonder she was murdered," Lady Lydia said.

"Lydia, that is most unkind," Lady Agatha said.

"It's a dangerous way to live," I told her.

"But who around here would have secrets worth the interest of a blackmailer?" Lydia said.

"I believe she collected her secrets from Dr. Forrester's medical records. I imagine an old country doctor would learn all sorts of damaging secrets about his patients," I said.

"But he would never have told," Lady Agatha said.

"Not him. All Mrs. Bryant had to do was sneak around the office, reading people's files while she was supposed to be working," Esther said.

"But now that she's dead?" Lady Agatha said. "Are

everyone's secrets safe now?"

"It's hard to tell," I said with a shrug. "Anyone who'd done 'business' with Mrs. Bryant would do well to tell the police before the police find out on their own."

"You think Mrs. Bryant kept some kind of record of who she was blackmailing and why?" Esther said.

"Not why, maybe, but who and how much. She'd need records of who still owed her each month. And the police haven't found those records yet. When they do…"

"What happens if someone else, someone in the village, finds her records first and understands what they mean?" Jane asked. She had entered into the spirit of the horror story we had pictured and her eyes were wide with the imagined carnage.

Lydia turned paler at the thought than her mother-in-law. "Oh, but the police wouldn't tell anyone what was in those records."

"No, but someone from the village might. Particularly if they gained access to Mrs. Bryant's house," I said, pointing out the difficulty.

"How awful," Lydia said with a shudder, setting down her tea cup.

"You don't have anything to hide, do you, Lydia?" Jane asked.

"No. Of course not." She strode across the room, hugging herself with her arms. "It's just—blackmail. How disgusting."

"I'm sure it's none of us," Lady Agatha said, glancing at me and then looking away. She'd seen how I'd looked over the family heirlooms. Was there something suspect about any of them?

"What I suspect about the secrets Mrs. Bryant learned is that, with a simple conversation, these secrets would no longer matter and wouldn't be worth anyone's attempts at blackmail," I said.

Jane shook her head. "It's surprising how people, anyone really, can be embarrassed over something affecting things that are unimportant."

"Such as status, you mean," I said.

"Faked educational honors from long ago. Parentage. An early liaison. A long-lost fortune from another generation. One child taking another's inheritance, such as jewelry or paintings," Jane suggested.

"Things that if they came out now would embarrass people but wouldn't put them in jail or shame them to the point they were run out of town," Esther said. "These things would be forgotten in a few days."

"That's easy for you to say," Lady Agatha said. "You are all newcomers to the village. And you're young. Status matters to some of us. When we are rooted in the community. When we are older and long settled in our lives and in the village."

"And perhaps we have more urgent uses for our money," Jane said through stiff lips. I thought again of the death duties.

"As long as no one finds Mrs. Bryant's notes, everyone should be safe," I said.

"And if they do?" Lydia asked.

"Then I suspect we'll be in for a long, bumpy ride."

"Is this what the police think?" Jane asked.

"Constable Bell has known Mrs. Bryant forever, and he thinks it's possible, but neither he nor Inspector Grimsby believe there is enough evidence to prove it," I said. "They think she angered someone enough with her spreading gossip around the village to kill her." I felt I should be honest with them. I hoped I'd learn more that way.

"Oh, please, let us talk about something more pleasant," Lady Agatha said. "Did you find enough clothing to fit your growing boy, Mrs. Redmond?"

"Yes, I did." And then I couldn't think of anything else to say, since I was trying to figure out who in the village would know where Mrs. Bryant would hide her little book of payments. With names.

"The clothing that would fit large four-year-old boys to small six-year-old boys was in shambles," Esther said. "Johnny outgrows his clothes so fast, and he is so hard on them. Multiply that by a half-dozen, and it was chaos."

Lady Agatha gave Esther a look of approval. "For a city child, he has taken to village life quickly."

"We've been here almost two years now," Esther said. "He's settled in. Hardly a city boy now."

We kept up the small talk for another ten minutes and then Esther rose, saying what a lovely time we'd had. I parroted her, my thoughts elsewhere.

As we moved toward the hall, I turned to study the family portrait one more time. I wasn't mistaken, it was the older boy with the gray eyes while everyone else's was light to bright blue.

"You seem transfixed by that painting," Lady Agatha said as she moved next to me. The others were already in the hall.

"Does Lydia know?" I kept my voice very low.

Lady Agatha's look was scathing.

"I'd better find that book. Who would know Mrs. Bryant's best hiding places?" I asked.

She hesitated so long I thought she wouldn't answer me. Finally, she said, "Mrs. Withins."

Lady Agatha and I exchanged a glance. I read in her look that she wanted her secret kept, and she had been paying to keep it quiet for many years. My only problem was I'd seen the dates on the knickknacks, and except for the possibility of Lady Agatha and the earl anticipating their vows by a bit, I couldn't see any reason to pay blackmail. Lady Agatha seemed to be too enamored with her reputation.

"Thank you so much for having us," I told her, and we joined the others in the hall.

"If the weather is decent, tomorrow afternoon I'm going to take Andrew for a walk as far as Oakley Rise. Care to come with us?" Jane asked.

"I'd love to," I replied. I mentally penciled in talking to Mrs. Withins for the morning. And Constable Bell for that evening.

Magda had made a cheese sauce out of practically nothing for that night's dinner and poured it over vegetables. Johnny pronounced them to be "very good vegetables" and Becca cleaned her plate without complaint.

I fed Stevie and put him down to sleep in time to meet Constable Bell as he made his evening rounds. "Good evening, Constable," I said as I went out our garden gate.

"Good evening, ma'am," he replied. "Had any more thoughts on our problem?"

"Yes. Mrs. Bryant must have kept a record in case someone failed to pay or got behind. I found someone who, while they didn't admit it, I believe had a secret they wanted to keep. Nothing criminal. Nothing that really matters. Something, however, that Dr. Forrester would have known. This person thinks there might be a secret book of payments in Mrs. Bryant's house, and Mrs. Withins is most likely to know where it is. I'm going there in the morning."

In the fading light, I saw Bell smile. "Hard evidence. Grimsby will be pleased if we get something—useful."

"Will you let me have the keys to the Bryant cottage tomorrow morning?"

He gave me a small salute. "I'll bring them round at breakfast time."

"Thank you, Constable." I watched him walk off and then heard footsteps coming toward me up the lane.

"Mrs. Redmond. How is the hunt for the killer going?" Mr. MacDonald asked in a cheery tone.

"Much too slowly," I told him. "What are you doing out so late?"

"I've been called back into work." When he saw my eyes widen, he said, "Nothing as frightening as an invasion. Just little bits of confusion."

"I'm glad to hear that."

"Goodnight, Mrs. Redmond."

"Goodnight, Mr. MacDonald." I turned and headed back to Esther's house when I heard a second pair of footsteps in the darkness. I hurried inside.

* * *

Bell was good to his word. The keys had been dropped off in the kitchen before I made it downstairs, Stevie on my shoulder. Setting him down on my lap, I sat and dug into my porridge and fake coffee. The bites Stevie had of the porridge thrilled him more than it did me. Remembering the wonderful breakfasts before the war, the real coffee and strong tea, I wished Hitler would choke on his that very morning.

"Stevie has a new outfit," Esther said as she handed me the newspaper.

"It's one I picked up at the Mothers' Union. It should fit him well for another month or two."

"Probably longer. His growth should slow down any time now."

"I'll be glad. He's getting heavy." I admit to sounding very proud, even as I complained.

Esther just looked at me, eyebrows raised, as I made my statement. She didn't believe me, either.

"Can you watch him for a little while after breakfast? I want to pay a call on Mrs. Withins before she and everyone else get going this morning, and I really don't want to take Stevie with me."

"This has something to do with Constable Bell dropping off a set of keys for you this morning?"

"Yes," I admitted.

"You'd better hurry, then. Nanny Goldie's already off with the children and I need to get to the shops this morning. I have no idea what Mrs. Withins has planned for her day. You've managed a rather late start, haven't you?"

"Yes." I gobbled down the rest of my breakfast without tasting it, kissed Stevie goodbye, and then did a fast job of getting ready to go out visiting.

I walked the short distance down the main street of the village and then down the side street to knock on Mrs. Withins's front door.

No answer.

"Hello? Is that Mrs. Redmond?"

I looked off to my right, up the side street, as an old lady in a housedress and cardigan walked across the front gardens of the house next door and then Mrs. Withins'. "Hello. Yes, I'm Mrs. Redmond."

"I thought so. I'm Mrs. Jenkins. I remember you from the WI meeting. It's that pretty auburn hair of yours. So like my Nellie's."

"Oh. Thank you. I'm pleased to meet you. Would you know when Mrs. Withins will be back?"

"No." The old lady shook her head. "But she's right over there. At Mrs. Bryant's. I saw her go over there this morning with some other woman."

"Who?"

"I don't know. She had her back to me, and her hat covered her hair."

"Well, if you'll excuse me, I'll just pop around and speak to Mrs. Withins."

I turned and began to walk toward the back door of Mrs. Bryant's cottage, expecting to find it open. And if it wasn't, I had the keys.

What I hadn't counted on was the old lady following me, although fortunately at a slower pace.

I rapped on Mrs. Bryant's back door and then tried to turn the handle. It moved and the door swung silently open. "Mrs. Withins? It's Mrs. Redmond."

I walked into the kitchen, aware somehow that the house wasn't empty. The air was cold and stuffy as I expected, and soundless, but the air felt disturbed, churned up. "Mrs. Withins?"

The drawing room was empty and looked undisturbed, while the bedroom was definitely disturbed. The wardrobe had been slid away from the wall and the mattress had been shifted half-off the bedframe.

The front door was closed but unlocked. As I started up the stairs, I heard the old lady who was still at the back door call out, "Is everything all right?"

"I'm not sure. Just wait a minute where you are." I climbed up to the first floor. On the left the bedroom was empty except for a bedframe, a wooden chair, and a large wardrobe. The furniture was coated in dust, although the floor had been swept recently. And then I found as I reached up and felt around that there was a small book on the top shelf of the apparently empty wardrobe.

Fortunately, I was relatively tall or I'd never have found the small black book I now held in my hands. Flipping over some pages, it was obvious this was a record of Mrs. Bryant's blackmail proceeds. I slipped it into my coat pocket and walked into the other bedroom.

And froze in my tracks at the sight of Mrs. Withins on the thin rug, blood bright against the faded green of the fibers. "Get Dr. Sampson or Constable Bell," I shouted down the stairs. "Whichever one you can find. Now!"

I heard the old woman scurry away.

Chapter Eleven

It must have been shock, because I began to feel faint and the room was turning gray. I sat down on the top step in the stairway, facing away from the body, and practiced long, slow breathing. Once I had my heartrate back to normal speed, I peeked back at the woman on the rug. Her eyes were unblinking and her open mouth was soundless. Her blood was not as bright as it had seemed at first. A trick of the light or of my surprise?

Another deep breath and I was able to look at Mrs. Withins. She wore a tweed suit with a pale pink blouse and low-heeled brown leather shoes. She was lying partly on her side and partly on her stomach, so I couldn't see the wound where the blood had come from.

Her gray hair was curly around her face, which I could see from the doorway, and she must have kept it long, judging by the thick roll or bun at the back of her neck.

I had to look beyond her. There were heavy blackout

curtains in the window and the bed was made up. This must have been Mr. MacDonald's room when he'd lodged with Mrs. Bryant.

"Is anyone here?" I called out, my voice weak.

Then I heard a door downstairs and heavy footsteps coming toward the front of the house. I gasped in fear before Constable Bell stepped around the corner to the bottom of the stairs.

"I think she's dead, but you might want to get Dr. Sampson." In response to my words, Bell climbed the stairs and I scooted on my bottom out of the way on the upstairs landing. I didn't feel quite ready to try my feet yet.

"What time did you get here?" he asked, taking off his helmet.

"Fifteen or twenty minutes ago. This was the last room I walked into. The woman next door…"

"Mrs. Jenkins."

"Told me when I knocked on Mrs. Withins's door that she had come over here with another woman whose face she didn't see. I was worried and came over here. Both front and back doors were unlocked."

"And Mrs. Withins was the only person you saw in here?"

"Yes. And I'm pretty sure she hadn't been dead long before I got here."

"Come along. I need to get you out of here, lock up, and get Doc Sampson."

I started down the stairs, holding on to the wall, when I heard the doctor's voice. "She's up here," I called. "No reason to hurry."

Once I made it down, Dr. Sampson went up, expertly I thought, for someone using a cane and carrying a doctor's bag. I heard him and Bell talking but I couldn't make out their words. "Mrs. Redmond, what time did you get here?"

"Less than half an hour ago now. At least twenty minutes. I'm sorry. I don't wear a watch and the clock here in the drawing room has stopped."

"No matter. I'd say you had a lucky escape. This woman has been dead a good deal less than an hour. I could easily be looking at two bodies now."

I looked up the stairwell in horror at Dr. Sampson's words, but he was back with Mrs. Withins; all I saw looking down at me was Constable Bell's shocked expression.

Once the two men joined me downstairs, the doctor continued. "Call Maudie Elliott for the body. In the meantime, Mrs. Redmond, you need to take more of your excellent photographs of the house again after the constable calls Inspector Grimsby."

When he reached the front door, he stopped and added, "You need to get a photo of her lying on her back after you take some as she was when you found her. There's a knife sticking out of her chest."

That explained the blood, I thought with part of my brain while I wondered at how matter-of-fact the doctor could sound.

"Let's lock up," Constable Bell said, reaching out for the keys in my hand, "and then you get your camera while I call Oxford and Maudie. I'll meet you back here in fifteen minutes."

I headed back to Esther's, thinking it was a good thing I'd received an extra roll of film. I was halfway back when a woman's voice said, "I just saw Dr. Sampson leaving Mrs. Bryant's house with you and the constable, but there's no reason to call them now with Mrs. Bryant dead. What's going on?"

Turning my head, I found Patricia Sharp walking beside me. She wore a blue, light-weight wool suit and a cloche hat. Too short to be a murderer, I thought. This was the woman I'd been told the village thought had killed her mother, Henrietta Johnson, on the path along the banks of the Wenmire. I'd also been told she had a perfectly good alibi, but since I'd just found a body, I was a bit nervous.

"You'll have to ask the police. It's not my place to say."

She walked beside me in silence for about ten paces before she said, "I didn't kill her. My mother. You don't have to be so afraid of me. No one does. If you don't think it's right to tell me, that's fine."

"I'm not telling anyone. Not just you," I replied.

"Oh, dear. Is Inspector Grimsby coming to Chipping Ford again?" Mr. MacDonald asked, suddenly appearing in front of us.

"I'm afraid so. Excuse me." Then I sped up to enter the garden gate and run up the short path to the front door.

I found Esther upstairs when I went up to get my camera with the new roll of film. This time I only had one photo of Stevie, smiling his gummy smile. She took one look at my camera and the expression on my face and said, "Taking more photos for Constable Bell?"

"Yes. He's called Oxford to let them know—about the current situation."

"Another body." Esther made it a statement.

"Yes."

"You found it?"

I shuddered. "Yes." At that point, my legs began to shake and I dropped onto the bed.

Esther sat next to me and gave me a hug. "We'll watch Stevie. You take care of your photographs for the constable."

"Thank you. I'll be back in time to feed Stevie lunch." Over my trembling, I rose and got my notebook and pencil as well as my camera and supplies and headed out the door.

After a few minutes' wait on the front doorstep, Bell let me in and we went upstairs. He and the doctor had set Mrs. Withins down other than the way I'd found her, so Bell and I rearranged her to match our memories of how we'd first found her. Then I photographed her before we rolled her on her back so the knife would be obvious in its current placement.

I climbed around to get various angles to show the damage that had been done, as I expected Inspector Grimsby would want. Only then did I widen my shots to show her position within the room and the distance to the door. Bell had come prepared with a ruler and not only did we use it to measure, we left it in one of the photos for the sake of comparison.

In the notebook, I wrote that I had been first on scene in finding the body and that both the front and back doors had been closed but unlocked. Then I took photos from the upstairs and downstairs halls, showing the stairs.

Then I took a few photos of the chaos in Mrs. Bryant's bedroom, and then of the kitchen and the drawing room to contrast how they were not disturbed.

What I made certain to show was that there were no bloody footprints or fingerprints anywhere in the room or stairwell. I photographed the front door handle after Bell pointed out a smudge we thought was blood.

The killer had stabbed two women without getting blood all over themselves. This little bit on the door handle downstairs was the first time we'd seen any sign the killer had been marked at all.

"I found out the coroner ruled the killer surprised Mrs. Bryant," Constable Bell said. "There were no defensive wounds."

"Did that seem to be true with Mrs. Withins?" I asked.

"I'll wait for the coroner again, ma'am," he replied.

"Do you know who I met in the street after you left?"

"Who?"

"Patricia Sharp. She seemed very interested in what I'd found in this house."

"What did you tell her?"

"To ask you."

Bell nodded. "Grimsby should be out here by midafternoon. I'll leave all the answering to him. But in the meantime, I'll let Maudie in and then start the house-to-house inquiries."

"I have the film and the notes, Constable. I'll bring them to Grimsby when he's ready."

He nodded to me as he let me outside, and I walked home to feed Stevie.

* * *

The rest of the day was sunny and pleasant, perfect weather for working in the garden, taking Stevie for a walk with Jane and Andrew, and talking to neighbors. This last was problematic, as the entire village already knew what had happened at Mrs. Bryant's cottage that morning and thought I should give them the details.

Mrs. Withins's neighbor knew enough to give everyone the bare bones of the story and the village had added their theories, suppositions, and assumptions, to the point that by after lunch they were all looking for Jack the Ripper.

Henrietta Johnson's younger daughter, Peggy Norris, a secretary for the MOD at the manor house, stopped at the garden fence on her way home from work to ask if it was the same person who killed her mother. Her suit looked newer than her sister's and she was obviously younger, but otherwise the two women looked alike, with short stature and brown hair.

I assured her I didn't know, and that she ought to ask Constable Bell if she wanted that information.

"Constable Bell?" she asked with a laugh. "He'll never figure this out."

"I hope he does. I don't want all of us living in Esther's house to be killed one night."

"Probably just one of Mrs. Bryant's blackmail victims," Mrs. Norris said.

"Are there any? I haven't met anyone willing to admit such a thing." And I would dearly love to meet someone in this village who'd be honest.

"In a village such as Chipping Ford? Of course, there are," she told me confidently, "but don't expect anyone to admit it." Then she strode off home, balancing on her high heels on cobblestones better than I would.

Did her mother, Mrs. Johnson, figure in with Mrs. Bryant's and Mrs. Withins's killings? The notebook I'd taken from Mrs. Bryant's house might give clues to who she was blackmailing, but that didn't explain Mrs. Withins's or Mrs. Johnson's deaths.

What had seemed so straightforward to me, a blackmailer killed by her victim, had now spiraled and rolled to include two women who had no obvious connection to Mrs. Bryant's sideline.

Or did they?

Constable Bell appeared on the road a few minutes later and asked me to bring my film and notes to the constabulary. I took Stevie inside and put him into the care of Magda until Esther came in from the garden where we'd been working. Then I cleaned up, collected my camera and notebook, and headed up the street to meet the police.

Inspector Grimsby was waiting for me, sitting on top of Bell's desk this time, where he fit much better. "I brought you something from Oxford."

Another fresh roll of film. I took the finished one out of my camera and put the new one in. Then I took out the pages of my notebook that corresponded with the discovery and the photos and put them on the desk.

My conscience wouldn't let me stop there. I removed Mrs. Bryant's small black notebook from my pocket and laid it on the desk with the other materials.

Grimsby leafed through it as he asked, "Where did you find this?"

"On a high shelf in the back of the wardrobe in the spare room at Mrs. Bryant's."

"Mr. MacDonald's room?" Grimsby sounded surprised.

"No. The unused room upstairs."

"Did you read it?"

I sighed and answered honestly, "I glanced at it."

"What does it show, sir?" Bell asked.

Grimsby slowly finished studying the notebook before he answered. "Three separate lines of income. Numbered one, two, and three."

Bell and I groaned in unison.

"The amounts and the time she'd been collecting from each one match what we found in her bank book. Two for a very long time, well over ten years, and one that starts not long before Mrs. Bryant was fired by Dr. Sampson."

"And there's no page where these three lines might have names?" I asked, hoping.

Grimsby shook his head. "Any idea who they might be?"

"I have an idea who one of them is, but she has a solid alibi and there's no reason why she would kill Mrs. Bryant now except maybe a little pride. It mattered more a year or two ago and before then in the past than it would now."

"I'll need to speak to her."

"Do by all means, but do it very quietly. If you don't press her for the reason, I think she'll be very honest with you. And she didn't do it." I stared hard at the inspector. "She couldn't have done it. She has a great alibi."

"Constable, if you'd do a patrol of the village, I'd appreciate it," the inspector said.

Bell stood, slapped his helmet on his head, and walked out with his back stiffly upright.

"He'll figure it out," I warned Grimsby.

"I know. Now who is this person?"

"Lady Agatha."

Chapter Twelve

I met Constable Bell on my way down the hill. "He should have let me hear who is suspected," he said. "I am a police officer. Unlike some." There was fire in his voice.

"It's not something that would be admitted to a man," I told him. "When Grimsby is gone, I'll tell you. He may tell you first, after he's interviewed her."

Bell seemed to soften a little at my words. "I'll hold you to that."

"I would expect you to. And if I told you this interview will go much better with an inspector than a constable, you'll have a pretty good idea where he is going."

"That's half the village," he grumbled.

"Think about it specifically, Constable."

"Lady Lydia," he said under his breath.

"Remember, the blackmail started long before Lydia set foot in this village."

Constable Bell paled. "I don't believe it."

"She didn't do it," I said.

"How do I know that?" He glared at me.

"At the time of Mrs. Bryant's stabbing, there was a minor flood in the back passage of the lodge. Jane and Lydia were cleaning out the gutter and mopping while Lady Agatha was walking the hall floor with Andrew where he could see his mother, since he was teething, croupy, or being generally bloody-minded and wanted his mother."

"If she had moved from that spot for an instant, everyone would have known," Bell said.

I nodded.

"All right. It wasn't her. It wasn't any of them." He stared at me. "So, it was one of the other two blackmail victims."

"I think so. And I don't know who they are."

"But we need to figure it out," Bell said and walked off.

I went home to find Esther hanging up the telephone in the front hall. "Guess who's coming for a visit tomorrow morning?"

Her smiling face told me. "Your father."

"And guess who's coming with him?"

"James."

She shook her head. "Your father."

"My father?" I had to sit down. He hadn't seen Stevie since he was two weeks old. He hadn't wanted to. In fact, he had thrown us out of his house. "How did Sir Henry manage that?"

"Maybe he reminded him of how much he loves you and

Stevie." Esther used her no-nonsense tone. "Maybe you need to remember that, too."

"He doesn't," I told her. "It's not that he dislikes us, he just doesn't know what to do with children. And with my mother not here to teach him, he retreats into silence. And don't forget, he hates noise, which children frequently create."

"Well, he'll be here tomorrow, so practice being gracious." Esther gave me an encouraging smile.

"Who's going to remind him to be gracious?" I asked.

* * *

The next day, Sunday, shone warm and bright. It was too nice a day to think about my father. Nevertheless, with the extra baking and extra polishing, we were obviously going to be honored with a special guest.

There was no way we'd make Sunday service. Apart from anything, we had no idea when they'd arrive.

I had both Stevie and myself dressed and ready for my father's inspection a good fifteen minutes before he was due. The more I fussed at Stevie's outfit, the more upset he became. Dr. Sampson's words came back to me. "Stevie can sense your tension and it makes him tense, too. Relax and he'll be fine."

I had been relaxed and he had mostly been fine. Until today.

Finally, Sir Henry's auto pulled up out front, no doubt causing a few people in the village to look out their lace curtains at the unexpected noise of a petrol engine on a Sunday. Private cars were seldom seen anymore due to petrol rationing, leaving the roads to bicycles, pedestrians, and the few commercial vehicles that might need to be out. Most of the farmers had put their horses back to work pulling delivery wagons, so the sound of horses' hooves were almost as common in the village as vehicle engines.

Johnny and Becca raced out to see their grandfather, while Esther, Stevie, and I followed sedately. Sir Henry climbed out and scooped both children up in a hug. My father came from the other side of the car and walked past the laughing children and up to—Esther. "So nice of you to invite me, Esther."

"Glad to have you, Sir Ronald."

Then he turned to me. "Hello, Olivia."

"Hello, Father."

He gave me a peck on the cheek. "Stephen certainly has grown."

"He has. He's been eating gruel and putting on weight."

"Gruel? Is that what babies eat?"

"One of the first things."

And then the conversation faded away.

Oh, no. I was not going to allow that. "How's the house?"

"Still standing."

"How's Mrs. Johnson?"

"Fine."

"Please tell her I've been thinking of her."

"I will."

I couldn't think of anything else and looked at Esther for help. "Would you care to come in for a cup of tea?" she asked.

"Thank you very much, Esther. That would be nice," my father replied.

Nine words. The most I seemed to get was two. I turned and walked into the house first. I led the way into the drawing room and sat on one end of the couch with Stevie on my lap. My father sat as far away from me as he could across the room.

"Sit with your daughter, Sir Ronald. You two have a great deal to talk about." Esther poured two cups of tea and set them by the couch before leaving the room.

My father rose and hesitantly took the other end of the couch. Was this so he could be certain I wouldn't hit him?

"Do you want to hold him?" I asked. "He doesn't bite."

"He doesn't have any teeth, does he?"

"He does, yes, these two bottom ones. Show Grandpa your teeth, Stevie." I made faces and grinned at him, which generally got him to smile back at me, showing his teeth.

My father craned his neck to see. "Oh, yes. So, what does he do all day?"

"He eats and sleeps and watches what Esther's children do. He laughs at the silliest things. He fusses and cries when his immediate needs aren't being met." I shrugged. "He's a very young baby. What did I do at this age?"

"I don't know. By the time I reached home at night, you were asleep." He looked at me in confusion.

"Adam has barely seen him. I hope when Stevie has children, Adam is not as frightened of them as you are of Stevie."

"I'm sorry." My father rose and paced the room. Stevie followed his movements. "I should never have come."

"It's good that you did." I gave him a weak smile. "It tells me that you care."

"Sit down in that chair, Ronald." Sir Henry had walked in without us noticing him until he spoke. He directed my father to a stuffed chair with a high back and arms. Once my father sat down, Sir Henry draped a couple of clean nappies over his suit jacket, shirt, and tie. Then he picked up Stevie from my arms and handed him to my father.

"No, bend your left arm at the elbow and hold the back of his head with your hand. Now put your right hand on his bottom. There, now keep a firm but gentle hold on him."

My father had a look of abject terror on his face, but he managed a pedantic "Firm but gentle?"

"You're doing fine. You're holding your grandson." Sir Henry looked proud of himself.

"Am I supposed to do anything?" my father asked.

"Is he crying?" Sir Henry asked.

"No."

"Then he's happy. You don't need to do a thing except

relax your shoulders a little. It'll be a few months before you can play with him. About the time he's crawling," Sir Henry said. He was warming to his school for granddads.

Then Johnny and Becca raced in, Esther behind them, and Stevie squirmed around to see them. My father tightened his grip, as if he was afraid he'd drop the baby.

Stevie let out a howl and my father started to rise and hold the baby away from his chest.

I leaped up and snatched Stevie into my arms, holding him so he could see Esther's children play with their grandfather. "As long as you are seated in that chair holding Stevie properly, there is no way you can hurt him. He could sense your tension and that's what he reacted to. It's okay. You'll learn," I told him.

"I'm afraid I'll hurt him long before I'll learn." My father looked ready to bolt and run, as if he were a spooked horse in a Victorian melodrama.

"You just need practice. Sit down and we'll try it one more time."

When he didn't move, I raised my eyebrows and he returned to his chair. I followed him and gently set Stevie into his arms again. This time I had him hold Stevie in a chair-like position against his chest facing out so Stevie could see Johnny and Becca without moving and frightening my father. His head and back were supported by my father's chest. Now my father didn't look quite so terrified.

I stood guard, but my father lasted a full five minutes,

even unbending so much as to talk baby talk to Stevie, who laughed and waved his arms, panicking my father again.

Then I reached over the back of the chair, pinning my father in place and helping support Stevie until my father relaxed into position one more time. It was short-lived, however.

Thirty seconds later, my father said in a weak voice, "Would you please take him back?"

Once Stevie was back in my arms, my father sighed loudly and collapsed into the chair.

"Well done, Sir Ronald," Sir Henry said from where he sat on the floor, Becca on his lap and Johnny hanging onto his back.

Esther, sitting on the couch, added her congratulations.

"I'm going to change him," I said, "and then if you'd care to, we can take him for a walk in his pram around the village."

My father nodded. "I'd appreciate that."

A few minutes later, we were strolling along the lane to the church. The parishioners were coming out from the service and some of them greeted us as they walked past, obviously curious about the identity of this strange man. My father tipped his hat to the ladies as he said, "You seem to have fit in here well with Esther. And your garden looks robust. You have a green thumb the same as your mother did."

I paused before continuing. He rarely mentioned my

mother or complimented me. What had happened? "Why did you come?"

"I didn't care for the way we left things when you moved out here, and a phone call didn't seem appropriate. In truth, babies frighten me. They make noise, they make horrible messes in their nappies, and I always feel less than adequate around them."

"And you were afraid I'd ask you to help."

"Yes."

At least that was truthful. "Then being here with Esther is the best place for Stevie and me to be. What do you think of the church?"

"Lovely. One of the Wool Merchant Churches? Stone walls, stained glass, and bell towers." My father was a fan of various architectural styles of churches.

I nodded. We walked around the village green, looked at the closed shops, watched some youngsters practice cricket, and ignored the village bobby, Constable Bell, coming in our direction.

"Hello, Mrs. Redmond," he said when he caught up with us.

"Hello, Constable Bell."

"Inspector Grimsby wants a word about that business yesterday."

"Constable, this is my father, Sir Ronald Harper. Father, this is Constable Bell. My father came out with Mrs. Powell's father and they'll be leaving after lunch, if Sir Henry sticks to his usual pattern," I told Bell. "There will be plenty of time for me to talk to the inspector after they leave."

"Olivia, have you become involved with the police again? Or is this more of Sir Malcolm's nonsense?" My father's face reddened in anger.

"Two local women have been murdered," I told him. "I've been helping out."

"Does Adam know you've been neglecting his son?"

All I could do was look heavenward and shake my head.

"She hasn't been neglecting the babe," Constable Bell said, shocked at his words.

"This is none of your business, Constable," my father said.

"None of yours either, I'd say. Mrs. Redmond's been out here how many months and this is your first visit?"

My father glowed bright red. He turned and marched back to Esther's house without a word to either of us.

"I'm sorry," the constable said, his face almost as red as my father's. "I spoke out of turn."

"Thank you, Constable. Don't be sorry for saying what needed to be said. Especially since I'd never say it."

I pushed Stevie back to Esther's and wheeled him through the front door to walk into a melee. "I'm staying for Sunday dinner, Sir Ronald. And I think Olivia would want you to stay as well," Sir Henry said.

"I would, Father," I said, "and so would Stevie."

At that point, Magda called out from the dining room

and everyone hurried in. Except my father, my son, and me.

"I can't get anything right, can I, Olivia?"

"Don't be maudlin. Just relax, and it will all work out all right. Just try to remember that our lives out here in Chipping Ford don't revolve around what you think." Personally, I wanted to see how my father did at a dinner table with two young children, a baby, and no newspaper to hide behind.

Chapter Thirteen

The answer was: my father did very well. For him.

Esther explained that Sunday dinner was the one meal of the week that we all made a point of eating together, including the nanny, the cook, and the children. It was the one meal of the week where we had a roast with vegetables and we all wanted to enjoy it immediately.

Sir Henry sliced, we passed plates around, and my father must have taken the constant disruptions in stride. This was one meal where his silence wasn't noticed. I was impressed that he didn't complain about the noise once.

Sir Henry asked for my newest column for the *Daily Premier* on raising children outside of London to save me having to mail it in, and I promised to give it to him after dinner. I asked how London was holding up under intermittent bombings and Sir Henry assured me the places I remembered were still standing and repairs were ongoing to the damaged buildings. Johnny asked his grandfather for a cricket bat. Esther immediately said no.

There was a pudding for afters with the coffee, and then Sir Henry and my father said their goodbyes. Esther and her children and Stevie and I walked out to the car with them. Before we reached it, my father stopped me.

"Er, um," he began as he pulled out his purse. "This should help you a little. I know children can be expensive. And if you wouldn't mind, I want to come out again and see you both."

Then he bolted for the car and climbed into the passenger seat.

I stood there with my mouth hanging open. My father had put a large number of shillings in my hand. When I got over the shock, I walked around to his window.

"Thank you for this. And I hope you do come out again. Especially since you know Sir Henry will be coming out, you can get a ride with him."

He spoke so quietly I could barely hear him. "Thank you."

* * *

After I put Stevie down for his nap, I went up to the police constabulary house. Grimsby was at the constable's desk again, looking as if he were an oversized stick figure. "Have a nice visit with your father?" he asked.

"Better than expected." It had been.

"Your film has been sent to Oxford. We should get it back tomorrow."

"Good. There's only one photo on that roll that I need to get back." He nodded and I continued. "What did you learn from Lady Agatha?"

He sighed and leaned back in the small chair. "There had been someone before the old earl. A rogue she had turned down. And despite this being Edwardian times, he got her alone and out of shouting distance of help."

"That poor woman," I said. "Dr. Forrester knew about it?"

"Yes. She had bruises, cuts, she had been beaten in her attempt to escape. Her parents called the local doctor, that being a very young Dr. Forrester, to hurry up to the manor. She was already engaged to the earl, she'd met him while he'd been in training, and her parents wanted the—difficulty hushed up. Servants were bribed. The rogue was threatened if he ever mentioned the incident."

"What did the earl say?"

"He never knew. He was wounded in France almost immediately after. Lucky for her. Her parents said she was ill and kept her away from everyone until the bruises and cuts healed. The wedding had already been scheduled. They just went ahead with it even though the groom was on crutches."

"Did she know?"

"She had her suspicions, but this was still the Edwardian era and young ladies were more sheltered then. Matthew was thought to be a honeymoon baby."

"And the earl never guessed?"

"He ended up with an heir and a spare and decided not to question his good fortune. Lady Agatha said he was a good deal older than her, with a first, childless marriage with a frail woman who died young."

"Why did Mrs. Bryant dig this out of Dr. Forrester's files? Lady Agatha could have denied it. Told her to peddle her blackmail elsewhere," I suggested. I would have.

"Dr. Forrester put all sorts of things into his medical notes. The name of the rogue and his description, which sounds similar to a description of Matthew as an adult. Dark hair and gray eyes. The doctor's guesses. Village gossip."

"No wonder Dr. Sampson didn't want us looking in Dr. Forrester's notes, if he was that indiscreet." I raised my eyebrows and the inspector nodded.

"I've also heard their alibi and I'm tempted to believe it," he said.

"Believe it. I've heard Andrew scream and it's not pretty."

Inspector Grimsby laughed, a full, rich sound that must have come from his toes. "A healthy lad. Good."

"And you? Do you have children?" I asked.

"Three children, five grandchildren. The boy is off with the army somewhere, as is one of my daughters' husbands, same as your husband."

When I didn't speak, he looked at me sharply. I nodded, pursing my lips together to hold in an unexpected sob. Then

I mentally shook off my pity party and said, "So, we know one of the blackmail victims and we agree she's not the murderer."

"Agreed."

"Do we have any idea of who the other two are?" I asked.

"I was hoping you could tell me that."

"Everyone else is acting normally. Or as normally as they do in this village. Can't we get into Dr. Forrester's records?"

Grimsby shook his head. "Dr. Sampson doesn't think it would be right to let us read the records and figure out who was being blackmailed. Particularly if we guessed wrong."

I cocked my head, remembering some burglaries I had done for Sir Malcolm. "How do you feel about breaking and entering?"

He made a face. "Let me get back to you on that."

"Until someone says something revealing or you find someone you want me to follow up on, I can't help you," I told him.

"Keep your eyes and ears open and we'll see what happens," he told me.

* * *

After the feast we had for Sunday dinner in the early afternoon, Sunday night supper was beans on toast, while Stevie had some very soggy toast. His, and ours, was dull and tasteless but filling. After we had the children settled in for the night, Esther and I sat in the drawing room with our tea and a couple of biscuits secreted away for just such times.

"Were you glad your father came out today?" Esther asked.

"Yes. I know it's amazing, and it may only be because we haven't seen each other in months, but we were both able to put in enough effort to get along. And he didn't drop Stevie," I added.

Esther laughed. "Yes, he scared me too at the time, but your father did get better at handling the baby."

"When will I ever get to see Adam?" I said. Well, yes, maybe I whined. James had been able to visit twice on weekends since we'd arrived. I admit I was jealous.

"Soon, hopefully."

"They're starting to send more troops to North Africa to open up another front. British, American, Canadian. I know Adam will be sent there to train troops or do some espionage. I just know it."

Esther patted my hand. "Two good things will come out of that, if it happens. Adam will get home leave before he's sent over, and the war will be over sooner with him involved in stopping the Germans."

"You're lucky James's expertise is in finance and transport. He's in Britain and will stay here, so he can continue to visit."

"It'll be all right, Livvy. Trust me." She took my hand and I squeezed it. If everything fell apart, I knew I could still count on Esther, and on a job with her father at the *Daily Premier* to provide for Stevie and me if Adam—no, I couldn't think about that.

I took a deep breath and let it out. I needed to think about something other than how much I missed Adam. "We've found out who one of Mrs. Bryant's blackmail victims is, but she's not the killer. We have two more to find. Any ideas?"

We had a fun time guessing. Frances Otterfield, the butcher's wife and WI chairwoman, along with Lady Lydia, were our first choices since they had been so nosy about the police investigation into Mrs. Bryant's death. However, we couldn't come up with a reason for blackmail.

Lady Agatha's friends, Mrs. Withins and Mrs. Brown-Dunn, were our next guesses, except Mrs. Withins had been the next one killed, and we couldn't come up with a motive for Mrs. Brown-Dunn.

We discussed various young farm-wives with young children, but none of them seemed to have a motive. We had as much trouble finding a reason for any of them to start murdering people as they would have in finding a motive for us.

"We don't know who killed Henrietta Johnson, do we?" I asked. "If she was killed."

"You think that is the reason Mrs. Bryant was murdered? Because she found out who did it?"

"It's possible. But barely," I said.

"One odd thing," Esther said. "Peggy Norris, Mrs.

Johnson's younger daughter. The one who wouldn't help take care of her mother. Do you know, she doesn't use Dr. Sampson? She said she had heard a rumor about him. Well, she thought it was about him. I wonder if it's possible that Dr. Sampson is one of the blackmail victims."

I considered the possibility. "Doctors have all sorts of ways to get into trouble, or to end up with families angry with them that start rumors. I need to talk to Peggy Norris to see what she knows about Dr. Sampson," I told Esther.

"She's a secretary for the MOD at the manor house. You can't get in there. You'll have to wait until you find her around the village in the evenings or weekends to talk to her."

"Which cottage is hers?"

"On the green, across from the shop with the post office. She has a few perennial flowers along the walkway and a good number of bushes in the garden she keeps trimmed."

"She can see who goes into the post office. Or at least the grocer's. That's a good way to know the villagers' business." I smiled. "I hope she enjoys gossiping."

"As long as you don't ask about her business," Esther said and raised her eyebrows.

We discussed Peggy Norris's work hours and when I might have a better chance to catch up with her on the lane along the green.

"Her son's a clerk in the town hall in Oxford a couple of

days a week and rides the bus to work. I've heard he has a medical deferment from the army. His heart."

"Won't they call him up for some office job in the army? Maybe working at the manor house?" I asked.

"Apparently not. I know Peggy was worried for a couple of years, saying no one was taking his heart condition seriously enough, but she seems reconciled to his status now. She seems pleased with his new doctor in Oxford. A heart specialist named Embleton. The boy is only allowed to work two days a week, which means the army doesn't want him at all."

I wondered how I'd react if I received that diagnosis for Stevie. I'd probably be in a panic until I learned what the symptoms were for an episode and how to manage it to keep him calm and get him through the worst of it.

When I went upstairs that night, I spent an extra amount of time listening to him breathe and being very grateful his breathing sounded even.

* * *

After the first post arrived in the morning, Constable Bell came down to give me the one photo of Stevie on the new roll of film. I'd already written to Adam the night before, so all I had to do was enclose the photo and take it to the post office.

Mrs. Norris, we'd noticed, always came back to her cottage at lunchtime when her son was in residence. I put Stevie in his pram and walked over to the post office with my letter at what Esther and I guessed was the correct time.

I met her in front of the post office as she started back to the manor house. "Oh, good. Mrs. Norris," I began, looking around and lowering my voice. "I heard you heard something off-putting about Dr. Sampson. Since Stevie needs to see him so often, I thought I'd better find out if I need to look elsewhere."

She scowled at me. "Where did you hear that?"

"Esther told me. Is it true? I need to take care of my little boy."

"I don't know. I heard a rumor." She tried to move around me as if we were in a dance.

"What was it?"

"I really must get back to work." Peggy Norris hurried around me up the hill, toward the entrance to the drive up to the manor house.

Determined, I nearly ran, pushing Stevie in his pram up the hill to keep pace with her. "It's important. Please. Do I need to worry? What was the rumor?"

She stopped near the gate and stared at me. "Look, you don't need to worry. The rumor I heard concerned Dr. Sampson and teenaged girls."

She rushed up to the gate then and showed her badge to the guard in army uniform. I turned around and headed back down the hill, stopping when I reached the police house. From where I stood, Mrs. Norris couldn't see me, since she'd gone up the path toward the manor house that

was hidden by the buildings along the lane.
 Good. I went into the constabulary.

Chapter Fourteen

I banged and struggled my way through the front door of the constabulary house with Stevie's pram and found Grimsby in his usual cramped position behind Bell's desk. "I have a possible person for the newest blackmail victim."

"Who?"

"Dr. Sampson."

"But… No. I can't believe it. He's respectable." He screwed up his face as he considered this.

"It's the rumor Peggy Norris heard about Dr. Sampson, that made her start using a doctor in Oxford. Apparently, he has a—liking for adolescent girls."

"Does he?" Grimsby raised an eyebrow.

"And considering the subject matter, you're the best person to talk to him about this. Does he even know that rumor is out there? Is it true?" Despite what I'd said to Mrs. Norris, I trusted Dr. Sampson. He'd done very well in relieving my fears as a new mother.

I should have guessed Inspector Grimsby would ask me a question along the lines I'd just been thinking. "He's Stevie's doctor. What do you think?"

"I trust him. But if that rumor is out there, there must be people who don't trust him, and he might pay blackmail to keep that rumor from spreading."

"I'll talk to him, but in the meantime, don't spread the rumor. We don't know what started it, do we?"

"I don't think it started here. Where is he from?" I asked.

"London."

"I wonder why he left. And does his cane have anything to do with it?" I remembered all the residential units that had collapsed under German bombs in the Blitz, including my own.

Then I pushed Stevie home so we could both get lunch and so Grimsby could get whatever information they had on Dr. Sampson at Scotland Yard. Once Stevie was down for his nap, I sought out Esther. She was getting a bundle ready to take to the laundry at the bottom of the village.

"I want to evaluate a rumor I heard that I don't believe, and I want to know if you've heard it." I helped bundle the children's clothes up.

"What?"

"That a man in the village has a liking for adolescent girls."

"Vicar. No. Dr. Sampson. No. Constable Bell. No. Bud the pub owner. No. Local auxiliary territorial army. No, none of those old men. Are there any other men in this village?" Esther asked me.

"Other than the workers at the manor house? No, and that answered my question. Thank you. Now, do you want me to help you carry this down the lane?"

After I warned Nanny Goldie that I was helping to carry the washing to the laundry and Stevie was in his cot, Esther and I walked down the road. When we got to the shed where Elfrieda ran her laundry business for the village, we found Jane there ahead of us. At least she'd had the sense to use Andrew's pram to carry the laundry, while we'd carried it in our arms.

Of course, Jane had as much to carry as we did, and I didn't see where she had any help.

"Ask Jane," Esther said when we finished putting our household laundry into barrels.

"Ask me what?" Jane said.

Seeing Elfrieda was listening, I tried to signal Esther to be quiet, but she said, "Do you know of any man in the village who has a liking for very young girls?"

"Nothing along those lines," Jane said, frowning.

"Harry. It was before any of your times," Elfrieda said. "He's been dead about ten years now. But back when, he had a liking for schoolgirls."

"Thank you, Elfrieda," I said. "That must be who they were talking about."

"Who?" Jane asked.

"A couple of the old ladies in the shops. I can't keep them straight." I didn't want to lie to Jane and Esther, but I couldn't think of anything else to say, and they were both looking at me oddly.

Jane and Esther talked for a couple more minutes while Elfrieda counted the laundry brought to her to give out receipts, but I barely heard them. No one had heard Peggy Norris's rumor in this village. Had she made it up, and if she had, why?

* * *

When we reached Esther's house, I made my excuses and walked home with Jane. "I want to speak to Lady Agatha, if she'll speak to me," I told her when we reached the entrance to the lodge.

Jane looked a little surprised, but she invited me in. "I'm back," she called once she'd shut the door.

"We're back here," came Lady Agatha's voice. I followed Jane to the kitchen, where Andrew was in his playpen and Agatha and Lydia were polishing silver at the kitchen table.

"I didn't know you were bringing home company," Lydia said, sounding embarrassed and flustered as she looked for a place to hide the polishing rag.

"Actually, I wanted to ask Lady Agatha about Mrs. Withins."

"Why?" she asked. I could see the suspicion in her eyes.

"We've had two people killed in this village, but Mrs. Withins seems as if she's an afterthought in the investigation. I didn't know her, but you did, Lady Agatha. What was she like?"

"A very respectable woman."

"Is that how you'd want her to describe you? Not as a loving mother and grandmother, a fine singer, a sharp bridge player, a—oh, I don't know. Mrs. Bryant has come alive during the investigation, but not Mrs. Withins. It doesn't seem fair somehow." I gave her a smile of encouragement.

Lady Agatha nodded. "She had a son and a daughter that she doted on. Spoiled a little much. She was a terrific needlewoman and led the group that did the altar cloths made in the 1930s. Her husband was a solicitor and an avid golfer, which suited her very much. He died not long before this war started. She loved to read in the evenings and always treated herself to the latest Christie or Sayers or Allingham. Does that help?"

"Very much. You've made her more vivid."

She studied me for a moment. "I'm glad to see you're not just in this for notoriety. That you care that my friend was killed. Do you think this will help you find her killer?"

"Honestly, no. I think Mrs. Bryant's killer thought Mrs. Withins might recognize her. But it helps to remember her as an individual and as someone's friend, not just a victim."

* * *

The rest of the day went along in its usual way, with letter writing, listening to the BBC on the wireless, making certain that no light showed from our property during the blackout, and taking care of Stevie, who chose that night to be fussy. Getting out of bed the next morning was a trial. There wasn't enough caffeine in what passed for coffee to keep me awake.

Nevertheless, I kept going.

I was ready to take Stevie for a walk when Constable Bell met me by our front door. "The inspector wants to speak to you."

"And I want to speak to him." We started off up the lane, Stevie enjoying the ride with the sun on his face, warm weather letting him wear lighter clothes, and room to kick in the pram. I was enjoying the sunlight and the oddly hot day for early in the season as well.

We walked along, saying hello to everyone we met and getting puzzled looks in return, until we, hurrying along, reached the constabulary.

Grimsby was inside waiting for us as we walked in, Bell and I maneuvering the pram through the doorway. "What did you learn?" he asked without greeting us.

"No one except Peggy Norris seems to have heard of the rumor she told me about." As my eyes adjusted to the darker interior, I realized there was a second person in the room. Mr. MacDonald.

"That's good," Mr. MacDonald said. "I spoke to the doctor last night."

"Yes?" I stared at Mr. MacDonald.

"I suppose you want an explanation of why I'm here,"

the older man said. "I knew Dr. Sampson during my time in London. At Scotland Yard. I'm retired, you see, but I couldn't sit on the sidelines with a war on."

"Are you doing something for the police at the manor house?"

"Something investigative, shall we say."

"That's enough questions for MacDonald. And you won't repeat the answers," Grimsby said. "And Dr. Sampson was livid that anyone could think that of him."

"I would think he was. He's a good doctor. He's been very understanding about my panic about Stevie."

Constable Bell gave a wave and headed out to patrol the village, and Mr. MacDonald followed him out, leaving Grimsby and me alone.

Grimsby scowled. "How did you question the gossips of the village?"

"I talked to a couple of my friends who hear more gossip than they share. And I didn't mention any names. I asked if they'd heard of any of the men in the village having an unusual interest in young girls. Turns out there was someone who's been dead for years. I learned that from a longtime resident of the village. They put it down to me listening to old-timers talking about old scandals."

"Good. I don't want you harming the doctor's reputation. And we've never solved Mrs. Norris's mother's murder. Or even decided if it was a murder. The inquest was quick and came back accidental."

"In other words, you'd question anything she told me?" I asked.

"I think she's still angry not to know what happened to her mother and as a result, she doesn't mind leaving the police to chase their tails. The coroner's verdict on her mother's death was accidental without any details." Grimsby shrugged, seemingly unable to decide what to do with anything Mrs. Norris said.

I nodded. "Everyone knows I've been helping you. But what did you learn from your police colleagues in London?"

"You mean besides MacDonald? Sampson is a dedicated doctor, serving the citizens in London and the troops back from France, until he was trapped in a building collapse at the beginning of the Blitz trying to help rescue someone. Once he got out of hospital, with lingering injuries from the building collapse, he came down here for a slower, easier practice. There's been no rumors about him either in London or here."

"What about his medical school?" I knew I was clutching at air.

"Once again, well respected, popular. There's nothing in his past to have earned him a bad reputation."

"I'm glad." I meant it too. "I think he's a good doctor. Coming here after Dr. Forrester had been in charge of the village for thirty years or a little more, he must have faced a lot of scrutiny. He's won over the villagers."

"Except for Mrs. Norris," Grimsby said, his tone dry.

"She's the only one I've heard of," I told him.

"So, we're still looking for two blackmail victims. One long-term resident of the village, one recent arrival."

"It doesn't have to be a recent arrival," I protested. "It could be someone who did something recently that was worthy of jailtime. An attack in the blackout, for instance. Or some noteworthy breech of the norms, such as the vicar having an affair with the postmistress."

"Someone who had been here for a long time, but only recently did something blackmail-worthy." Grimsby nodded, considering it. "But there hasn't been anything that fits, has there?"

"Other than the questionable death of Mrs. Johnson? Not that I know of. And I certainly haven't heard any rumors about the vicar." I almost started giggling. The vicar was in his mid-fifties and well looked after, and watched, by his wife. Having heard his sermons, I didn't think he had the imagination to have an affair.

"We keep coming back to the death of Mrs. Johnson. And yet something else happened here a long time ago besides the scandal we know about," Grimsby reminded me.

"I'll let you know if I discover anything else," I told him and walked home, Stevie stirring from his nap as his pram rocked him along. I wasn't the only one who'd missed sleep the night before.

I returned home to find out at least one postal delivery had arrived, and with it, a letter from Adam. "It's a letter from your papa, Stevie," I told him and then began to read. "Oh."

"What is it?" Esther asked, coming in from the kitchen.

"Adam is getting family leave, followed by a long journey."

We stared at each other for a full minute before Esther took my hand. "The sooner they start sending people such as Adam out into the field, the sooner this war will be over. He's welcome here as long as he can stay," she told me.

"I hope they aren't sending him to Russia." My lower lip quivered, followed by tears welling up in my eyes.

"I wouldn't think so," Esther said breezily and then saw on my face how little I appreciated her easy confidence. "You'll find out when he gets here. Nothing you can do until then. When's he coming?"

I told her and then headed out with Stevie and my letter. Adam's background in intelligence as well as in training told me they could be sending him to Russia, to Norway, to Egypt, to Jerusalem, to Malta, to Gibraltar. I didn't care for the sound of any of them.

Oh, how I wanted this war over.

There was an old bench past the bridge over the stream. Half hidden by trees, it overlooked a beautiful view of the brook. I wheeled Stevie off the lane and over to the bench where I sat, sunk in misery. Tears blurred my view of the Wenmire while Stevie slept peacefully.

I didn't hear anyone approach until Frances Otterfield

said, "Did you lose someone?"

I wiped my eyes, but I couldn't face her yet. "No. This is fear that I will."

"Your husband is in the army."

"Yes."

Mrs. Otterfield sat down beside me. "You're lucky you have your baby to focus on while he's away."

I looked at her sharply. "Would that work for you?"

"It would if we'd been blessed with a child."

I shut my eyes against my insensitivity and nodded. "They are wonderful, but they aren't the be-all and end-all we tend to think."

"Imagine how much darker your world would be right now without him."

"On balance, I think I'll keep him," I said and we both laughed. "Seriously though, was there nothing doctors could do for you and your husband? Or adoption, perhaps…"

"It was a doctor who caused the problem, years before I met my husband." She picked up a stick and heaved it into the stream. "All because my mother would have been ashamed."

"Your mother would…?" I looked at her, puzzled. It made no sense. And then all of a sudden, it did. I felt my cheeks heat at my insensitivity.

Mrs. Otterfield leaped up from the bench. "Forget I said anything."

"You didn't say anything except you wish you had a

child. No shame in that," I told her.

"Yes, well, I'd better get going. You have a handsome little one." She strode out to the lane and then continued on away from the village.

"Thank you. Good day," I said after her, but I doubted she heard me.

What a strange and embarrassing conversation. That made me think it might have something to do with Dr. Forrester and Mrs. Bryant and blackmail. The Otterfields, I had learned, had been in the village and their farm outside of town forever. If Mrs. Otterfield had a secret in the doctor's files, she could be one of the long-term victims, the same as Lady Agatha.

If Inspector Grimsby would let me break in, I knew exactly where to look in the medical files.

Chapter Fifteen

I went back to Esther's ready for dinner. I wasn't hungry, I was too upset about Adam's transfer, but I was ordered by Esther and Magda to sit down and eat. "They won't send your husband to Russia," Magda assured me. "They have been fighting there for nearly a year, correct?"

"Yes."

"And the Russians are very much in charge of this war on their doorstep, right?"

I nodded my agreement.

"Well, Esther says he is very talented in finding out what our allies are planning so Britain can get the best results from working with them. We are not working with the Russians, they are fighting alone in their country. He would be wasted there." She spoke as if this explained everything.

I wanted to know what Esther had told her. Adam's spying was supposed to be a secret. I gave her a dark look, but she merely smiled at me. "They wouldn't send him to

Norway, since his legs haven't healed enough for him to get around on skis. They've been fighting over Malta for two years now, and that's all British naval and RAF forces, so he's not going there. Either Gibraltar to find out what the Spanish plan, or Egypt to find out what the North Africans can be called on to do." Esther popped another bite of dinner into her mouth, new potatoes and peas, and nodded at Magda.

"It's very good," Esther said after she finished her bite.

"You think so?" I said. Seeing the cook's thunderous expression, I added, "Not the dinner, that is very good, Magda. No, Adam's assignment."

"You'll find out when he gets here, so don't worry in the meantime. It's your turn to do dishes tonight, Livvy. Don't forget," Esther told me.

"How could I? You won't let me," I said and gave a dramatic sigh, the back of my hand against my forehead in melodrama fashion.

* * *

The next morning, as soon as I finished my chores and Stevie was settled down, Constable Bell showed up on our front step as if he'd timed his arrival to my schedule.

"Grimsby's bosses want him back in Oxford since he's not making any progress with either of our murders," he told me.

"They'd just leave us with a murderer loose in the village?" I asked.

"They have more than enough crime in Oxford alone to

keep their entire force busy. The countryside is going to have to fend for itself," Bell said.

"I wonder if Grimsby is ready to let us break into Dr. Forrester's records now. I know someone who could well be the other long-term blackmail victim, but she's no more a killer than the first one."

Bell stared at me. "You know who the second victim is?"

"Maybe. I think so from something she said yesterday, and she's very frightened of anyone learning her secret. I don't know her alibi for the times of the murders, though."

Nanny Goldie came up to us and said, "I'm taking both children to the green to play. Do you need me to take Stevie as well?"

"You're a lifesaver. Thank you." I made certain Stevie was settled in his pram and then Bell and I hurried off. Within a couple of minutes, we were at the constabulary house, but Grimsby was nowhere to be seen.

"He's been staying at the pub," Bell said, and we walked along the path until we reached the back door of the pub. Bell marched in without hesitating and I followed him.

"Here for the inspector?" Bud, the landlord, asked. Middle-aged, he was a member of the home guard in case we were invaded, but his instincts, I was certain, would lead him to invite the Germans back to the pub for a pint, making sure to charge them double what he'd charge his regulars.

Come to think of it, Bud would make the perfect decoy, leading the Germans back to the pub, a smile on his wide face, while the rest of the home guard awaited in ambush.

"Yes, is he here?" I asked.

"Just finishing his breakfast. Come in and have some coffee."

"I don't have any money on me," I said with some regret, since pubs got a better grade of what passed for coffee than we could get in the shops.

"I'm sure the police budget can run to another cup of coffee," Bud said cheerfully.

"I've been given one more day," Grimsby said, looking skeletal and disheveled as we walked up to his table.

"We need to discuss this at your office," I said.

"You have something," Grimsby said, smiling as he rose from the table. "Let's go."

"Your breakfast," Bell and I said in unison, looking at his half-eaten plate.

"I'm finished. Let's go."

Bud came over with two cups of coffee and set them down on the table. "Now, Inspector, you wouldn't want to upset my lady wife, now would you? So finish your breakfast while these two helpers of yours have a cup of coffee."

Bell gestured Grimsby to sit down, which he did.

"Better than I get at home," Grimsby muttered.

"She's a good cook, is Brenda. Doesn't explain…" Bell's voice drifted away.

"What?" I asked.

"Constabulary," Bell replied.

When we finished, Grimsby led the way down the path to the constabulary house, where he took his favorite spot behind Bell's desk.

I gave him a general report of my conversation with Mrs. Otterfield without mentioning any names, ending with "No one here knows anything of whatever happened and she is desperate to keep it that way."

"Obviously, a prime target for a blackmailer," Bell said.

"Without knowing exactly what happened, I won't be able to pin her down and neither will you. We need access to her medical records," I told Grimsby.

"I tried this sort of situation on Dr. Sampson and he said absolutely not."

"How do you feel about breaking and entering?" I repeated the question I' posed on Sunday, hoping Grimsby would finally approve. And if he was leaving the village, that night was our last chance.

"It's wrong." He sounded quite firm about that.

"No one is arguing that. But how do you feel about going in after office hours and reading old files?" I gave him a little smile.

"You're certain she's the one being blackmailed?"

"As certain as I can be until I see the file. The file Mrs. Bryant must have read."

"Do you know how to break in without getting caught?"

My face reddened then. "I don't know how to break in, precisely. My skill is in going through the files quickly and finding the information we need to get this woman to admit she was being blackmailed."

"And our killer?"

"I don't think she's the one." I stared at Grimsby. "Somebody is. Finding out about this woman will help narrow things down, I hope."

"And I have one more day." He shook his head. "This is a bad idea. But if I can get you into the office, can you take it from there?"

"Yes." I spoke with more assurance than I felt. "Now, Constable, what were you thinking of in the pub?"

"Bud's wife, Brenda, gave him a bad case of food poisoning once. Fortunately, Bud sampled the dinner before it was served to any of their customers. Caused a lot of excitement at the time."

Fortunately, I didn't eat in the pub. And I didn't see how this could link to our blackmail murders.

"I finally heard from Manchester," Grimsby said. "Dr. Forrester's daughter, who'd had the arguments with Mrs. Bryant. They were all on the same subject. Mrs. Bryant wanted her position at the doctor's surgery guaranteed. The daughter said no. And she was in Manchester at the time we asked about."

* * *

I was on pins and needles the rest of the day. I couldn't focus on anything, so I kept my activities to that which I could do in my sleep, such as changing nappies and weeding the garden. I had no idea what we ate for lunch or dinner, but I did notice I cleaned my plate.

After we listened to the wireless, I fed Stevie and put him down for the night. Then I changed into dark clothes and told Esther I was going out and not to ask any questions.

"Tell me when you return so I can stop listening for Stevie," she said and turned back to the book she was reading.

I went out and put the door on the latch. Keeping to the edge of the lane, I headed in the darkness of the blackout for the doctor's surgery, avoiding the side of the building where the doctor lived.

When I reached the door to the surgery, a dark figure stepped out in front of me. I took a step back and ran into the railing as a voice whispered, "It's me. Bell."

"Where's Grimsby?" I hissed.

"At the constabulary. I've unlocked the door."

We went in, every board that squeaked sounding as loud as an artillery shell. I took Bell's torch and went to the file cabinets in the far corner of the office where Dr. Forrester's patient notes were kept. Fortunately, no one in this village thought to lock up anything, unlike in London, and I found the Otterfield files in less than a minute.

"It's what I suspected."

Bell came and read over my shoulder. "As much as they want a baby now, to destroy their chances back then. Shame."

"She was just a child herself at the time. Sixteen. The father was a single man, a student who frequented her father's pub and wouldn't admit to what he'd done. And her mother was ashamed. A recipe for disaster. Poor woman. She's paid a terrible price for something that wasn't her fault." I was angry on her behalf. Blackmailed for what others had done to her, while those who'd hurt her suffered no consequences.

"Apparently, Jim Otterfield doesn't know any of this," Bell said.

"And you will make sure it stays that way, Constable," I replied.

At that moment, a telephone somewhere in the doctor's living quarters rang.

"It'd do no one any good for this to get out now. Let's go."

While I put the file away, Bell took the torch and headed for the door. I shut the file drawer and turned around, unable to see anything around me. "Bell!" I whispered.

I put my hands out to feel anything before I tripped over it and began to walk toward where I saw his figure standing by the door, torch pointed at his feet.

I hit the desk with my left leg and hip and nearly fell over. As I balanced myself on the desk, my hand swept the desk lamp onto the floor, shattering the light bulb and the glass shade.

The crash was an unholy noise, splitting the silence. Bell

shone his torch over the damage, a look of horror on his face. Then he stepped out of the doorway into the night.

There was nothing to do but run. In the darkness, I hit the door, but the cooler air told me where the doorway was, and I was outside in an instant, shutting the door after me. Then I hurried away in the opposite direction from the doctor's living quarters so the surgery would hide me as I escaped. My dark clothes helped, too, I decided, as I saw a light come on in the surgery and a moment later the outside door opened.

I hid behind a bush, unmoving, until the shadow of Dr. Sampson disappeared back into the surgery. Then I crept along the long way around to the police. Fortunately, there was a little light from the quarter moon to guide me so I didn't trip and fall outside.

Bell and Grimsby were waiting for me.

"Couldn't you leave without wrecking the office?" Bell asked.

"Couldn't you hold the torch so I could see to get to the door without running into anything?" I asked in return.

"You need to move faster."

"I could have if you had given me a little light to move by."

We faced each other, our voices raised, until Grimsby said, "Enough."

We both turned to him. "The damage was unfortunate, but neither of you were seen. And you have a good candidate for the other long-term blackmail victim."

"Bell told you her secret?" I asked.

"Yes. Only sixteen. Her parents probably didn't believe her. And then to be left damaged and unable to have any more children. Poor woman." Grimsby shook his head.

"And I think she fears her husband finding out why they don't have children," I said. "He'd be the only one she'd truly fear learning her secret after all these years."

"Makes her an easy target for Mrs. Bryant and her long-term blackmail. And a butcher shop has a lot of cash moving through it. Mrs. Otterfield could get a small amount out to pass on month after month without getting caught," Bell said.

"Then I'd better talk to her before I go back to Oxford," Grimsby said.

"She didn't do it," I told him.

"You've said that, and she was in her shop in front of customers when Mrs. Withins was killed. The only reason to kill Mrs. Withins was because she knew who killed Mrs. Bryant."

"Or she planned to start up Mrs. Bryant's blackmail business," I said to Grimsby.

"I still need to speak to her. Clear away the underbrush. But you need to keep your eyes and ears open. The killer is still out there." He pointed a bony hand at both Bell and me. "No bickering. I'll do what I can from Oxford, but you two will have to work together if the killer is to be caught."

"Let Bell know what you learn from Mrs. Otterfield and then he can pass it on to me. Right, Constable?"

"Hmmm."

He didn't sound very willing to me.

Chapter Sixteen

I passed Constable Bell while I was pushing Stevie in his pram in the weak sunshine the next afternoon. "Good afternoon, Constable."

"Afternoon, Mrs. Redmond." He stopped but he didn't say anything more.

I raised my eyebrows.

"Inspector Grimsby has left town. Before he did, he spoke to Mrs. Otterfield. She had a good alibi and swears she didn't kill anyone, but Mrs. Bryant was bleeding her dry. That she admits."

"Who does she think killed Mrs. Bryant?"

"A public-spirited individual and she hopes they get away with it."

"Hardly fair to Mrs. Withins," I said.

Bell nodded. "That's true enough."

"Did Grimsby learn anything of any use to us?"

Bell shook his head.

"Let me know if you hear anything new."

"You do the same." Bell walked away, whistling.

I hoped the constable sincerely wanted to get along with me for the sake of the investigation and the village.

The next few days passed in relative peace. My father and Sir Henry planned to come out on the following Sunday. I was counting down the days and weeks until Adam came home on extended leave before he went overseas.

I cleaned and worked in the garden in between changing nappies and feedings. In the evening we listened to the radio or read. We attended the WI meeting with the topic of "Mending and Making-do" on sewing, something I'd always preferred to pay someone else to do for me. I could sketch my ideas, but my stitches always looked hurried. They were hurried, because I was bored sick before I started.

That gave me an idea. I contacted the seamstress who had made most of my clothing before the war and had adjusted many of them for me when I was pregnant. Now I needed everything put back to my current size. The seamstress said if I could bring things in and let her measure me, she could send my clothes back by post.

The next morning, I fed Stevie at dawn and then left Esther and Goldie with directions for his care during the day. This would be a long, uncomfortable day for both Stevie and me, with no time to dawdle. Then I caught the first, early bus to Oxford and the train from there into London.

My first stop was at the bank to make a cash

withdrawal. Then I went to the seamstress with a suitcase full of too-large clothing and the money to pay for her work. By one o'clock, I was done and could catch an earlier train to Oxford.

I started walking through the grubby, gloomy, bomb-damaged streets of London toward the train station. Everywhere there was the smell of petrol and smoke and ashes and the scars left by explosions. I felt right at home. I was more than halfway back to the train station, avoiding a particularly large crater, when I heard my name called.

I turned to find Mr. MacDonald hurrying to catch up with me. "What are you doing in London?" he asked.

"Errands that couldn't be put off any longer. And you?"

"Meeting with some old work colleagues in Scotland Yard." I noticed he didn't say why. I guessed it was related to what he was working on at the manor house. "If you have time before we have to catch the train back to Oxford, would you care to have lunch?"

"Very much so." This was turning into a treat despite the stuffy, stressful rigors of wartime travel.

We ate in a fish and chip place, special because Magda never fried fish or potatoes and because our conversation wasn't interrupted by small children. It was terrific to have such a change. We discussed blackmail, murder, and the gossips in our village without having to tone down our words for small listening ears.

"Has Grimsby found the killer yet?" Mr. MacDonald

asked.

"No, and if his bosses don't stop pulling him back to Oxford he may never find our village murderer," I said. "I don't know how long it's been since I had fish and chips. Thank you for suggesting this."

"I found this place years ago when I was working at Scotland Yard. I'm glad it's still in operation."

"This is what we need in Chipping Ford," I told him with a smile. I didn't realize how much I'd missed such a simple dish.

"I don't think they'd do enough business to keep it open," Mr. MacDonald said. "Has Grimsby found any of the blackmail victims?"

"The two long-term ones. Neither one could have killed Mrs. Bryant because of their alibis. We have no idea who the short-term victim is, though. Perhaps that's our killer."

"It makes more sense," Mr. MacDonald said. "Someone who's been paying blackmail for ten or twenty years isn't suddenly going to murder their blackmailer, are they?"

We rode together on the train to Oxford, standing all the way, and then Mr. MacDonald walked me to the bus stop to catch the last bus to Chipping Ford. I arrived home to find my little man was hungry and Magda had saved some dinner for me. After Stevie was fed and put to bed, I exchanged gossip with Esther about London shops and blackmail in our village.

One thing I didn't hear was any gossip about breakage

in Dr. Sampson's surgery. I began to think I'd dreamed it until, at the end of the week, Constable Bell came in the garden gate and walked to the side of our vegetable patch.

I rose from my knees. "Hello, Constable."

"Mrs. Redmond." He walked over and said in a low voice, "Dr. Sampson is certain we broke into his office and broke the lamp. He wants two pounds in restitution and won't say anything more about it. One pound each?"

"Fair enough. My father's coming out Sunday. I'll get my share from him." While I'd been at the bank, I had taken out money for the seamstress, postage for letters, and my share of the housekeeping with Esther, but I hadn't thought to take out extra to pay for the lamp.

"Don't you get any money from your husband?" Bell sounded confused.

"Adam keeps a certain percentage for his expenses and sends the rest to the bank in London, where I draw out an amount for rent to Esther and expenses for Stevie and me when I go into London. So far I've only gone to London once since I arrived here, just the other day, and I need to make that money last as long as I can."

"Why not have your father bring you money from your account?"

I gazed at Bell as if he'd blasphemed. "There is no way I'd allow my father into my bank account. But he brought me some money when he came out to visit before. Sort of a bribe."

"He bribes you to see him?"

"He threw us out of the house when Stevie was two weeks old. He did us a favor, really, but I think he feels guilty."

"Threw you out? How is that a favor?" Bell sounded as if he thought we were both crazy.

"He called Sir Henry, Esther's father, about Esther taking us in before he threw us out. Sir Henry and Esther had both been to visit and had agreed between themselves that the baby and I needed to leave my father's house."

"What is so bad about your father's house? Is it falling down?"

"No. He just can't stand any noise at all. He wants quiet at all times. I don't know what he did when I was a baby."

Bell shook his head, his eyes wide. "I'll see you after he leaves on Sunday."

As he started to walk away, I asked, "Have you heard anything of our third victim?"

"Nothing. Have you?"

"No. Nothing." Drat. I had hoped he'd solved the murders already.

Saturday was spent scrubbing everything so that it would shine on Sunday for the arrival of my father. At one time or another, Esther, Magda, and Nanny Goldie told me to relax, things were clean enough, and I needed to stop worrying about my father's opinion.

I wished I could.

Sunday dawned bright and warm, the first day of summer, or at least it felt that way. I dressed Stevie in a cute little set of shirt and short trousers that I had picked up at the clothing swap the Mothers' Union had held. I wore a lavender summer frock I could barely fit in at the end of last summer since Stevie had already been making his presence known. Looking in the mirror, I knew I had lost weight, and not just baby weight.

Then I looked at Stevie and realized what I had gained. And felt sorry again for Frances Otterfield.

The sound of a car in the lane, a sound we seldom heard with the petrol shortage, warned me my father and Sir Henry had arrived. By the time I walked downstairs carrying Stevie, Johnny and Becca were already outside climbing on Sir Henry while Esther watched, laughing.

I walked out the front door with my son in my arms and directly toward my father. He smiled at his grandson and gave him one of his fingers to grasp. "He's got a good strong grip."

Sir Henry must have taught him that trick. He hadn't tried to give Stevie one of his fingers the last time he visited.

Neighbors started to walk up the lane toward the church, waving to us as they passed. My father tipped his hat to a couple of them. Sir Henry disappeared on the other side of the auto under two squirming, shrieking grandchildren.

Patricia Sharp passed us at speed, red in the face, while her younger sister, Peggy Norris, called after her, "Don't run away from me, Patricia." At the same time, Peggy tried to hurry up a young man and a teenaged girl I thought were her children. The male, who was a little pudgy, was breathing hard as he tried to catch up to her. The girl, who was a few years younger, kept her distance and looked as if she didn't want to admit she knew either of them.

Jane Fletcher, who pushed Andrew past the church to say hello and meet our fathers, shook hands with my father while I gave them their proper titles. My father looked shocked for a moment before he gave a bow from the neck and said, "Lord Andrew."

"Oh, please don't," Jane said. "He has to get through primary school before he needs to deal with the other boys teasing him over his title."

"Unfortunately, he has the title and he needs to grow up used to the idea. I'm Lady Agatha Fletcher," Jane's mother-in-law said as she held out her hand to my father.

"You're this stout fellow's grandmother?" my father asked. "You must be very proud of him."

I thought I saw Agatha wince at being called a grandmother, but I leaped into the hole and introduced her to my father. They carried on the social pleasantries for a couple of minutes, agreeing on the weather and the beauty of the village, while Jane and I discussed the play on the radio the night before and how we imagined the characters were dressed.

Lydia arrived then and nearly dragged the other two

ladies into the church.

My father said, "Are we keeping you from attending?"

"No, we don't get to spend much time with our fathers, so Esther and I are happy to miss an occasional service. Especially the sermons," I added quietly.

My father, Stevie, and I sat on the bench in the back garden and watched while Sir Henry, Esther, and the older children played tag and rolled in the grass. We heard the congregation leave the church while we were in the back of the house, so the voices were muffled. They had a warm, communal hum similar to a distant hive of bees.

Finally, Magda called us in for a delicious Sunday pot roast with lots of vegetables. We all enjoyed it immensely, including Stevie, who chewed on a small piece of potato that he kept pushing out of his mouth with his tongue while trying to eat it.

I noticed my father didn't try to hold Stevie on this trip, but he sat next to us and let Stevie grab his finger or his sleeve, talking to the boy the whole time. He even asked me a few questions about Stevie and how we were getting on.

I was amazed at how much effort my father was putting into this visit. Or how much advice Sir Henry had given him.

At the end of dinner, Sir Henry pulled me aside. My father frowned but let Stevie and me go. Sir Henry said, "I've been looking into some backgrounds for you, and your Dr. Sampson might have some explaining to do."

"Oh?" Could Peggy Norris's story be true after all?

"The house that crushed him was his neighbor's. A jeweler by trade. Supposedly, there were cases full of diamonds and precious stones and gold in the house, but those cases were empty according to the rescuers. True, they may have been taken by thieves, but it could also have been your doctor. And he took his doctor's bag out of the wreckage to hospital with him, so he had a way to remove the jewels."

I didn't want to think of Dr. Sampson as a thief, but Sir Henry built a strong case for it. I sighed and said, "Do you want my column now?"

"If you have it ready for me."

I did.

Before the children had to take their naps, my father and Sir Henry said farewell and we walked them out to the car. Again, my father gave me some money, this time including a couple of pound notes. I thanked him without telling him why I was so grateful.

We waved the grandfathers goodbye and then came the difficult process of settling down tired, excited children for their naps. I came downstairs after Esther did to find Constable Bell in our hall.

"I thought you might want to go over to Dr. Sampson's with me," the constable said.

"Let me get my hat and gloves," I said and went to fetch them. Once I was ready, I told Esther I was off again for a short while and to keep an ear out for Stevie.

We found the doctor at home, listening to the radio in his stocking feet. "Please excuse me for having my shoes off. It's easier on my feet and my legs," he said as he ushered us into his drawing room. "I apologize for greeting you so informally."

We both declined tea but took seats. The doctor looked at us expectantly.

"Constable Bell tells me the lamp we broke cost two pounds. We've come to pay our shares." I handed him a pound note, now slightly damp from my sweating palm. Bell followed me in handing over his money.

Dr. Sampson scowled. "What were you doing to break my lamp?"

"A patient of yours, and Dr. Forrester's, said something to me that told me she must have been a blackmail victim of Mrs. Bryant. The patient didn't make clear why, so we checked her ancient records where Mrs. Bryant would have learned the woman's secret. We didn't think she killed Mrs. Bryant, and she couldn't have, but we needed to have the inspector question her to clear her of any suspicion."

"Couldn't you have done this without reading my medical files?"

"I'm afraid not. But now we have the two people who were blackmailed but couldn't have killed anyone removed from suspicion. They both have solid alibis."

"And I suppose you want back into my records." Dr. Sampson sounded frosty.

Bell shot me a look when I said, "Not necessarily. If Mrs. Bryant found a reason to blackmail you, it wouldn't be in your records."

"What?" Dr. Sampson forced a laugh. "How would Mrs. Bryant find out anything about me, if there had been anything to find?"

"I don't know how she'd find out, since the official story is you were injured when a building fell on you while you were rescuing trapped people. But that isn't what really happened, is it? At least, that's not the whole story." I looked into his face but he didn't return my gaze, telling me Sir Henry's information was accurate.

The constable looked puzzled. When he moved to say something, I held up a hand. He gave me a searching look but then nodded.

"As far as Mrs. Bryant knew, the official version was correct. She never tried to blackmail me." Dr. Sampson still didn't look at either of us.

"I'm glad to hear that. I want to hear you say you didn't kill her."

"Of course, I didn't kill her. I believe in the Hippocratic oath," he snapped at me.

"But your oath doesn't preclude you from stealing from bombed-out houses," I said.

I saw understanding dawn on Bell's face.

"The house that was bombed was my neighbor's. I knew he was quite rich. I went in to get anyone out to safety that

I could. The house was barely standing and was going to collapse before help arrived. I checked and they—the man, his wife, their daughter and their maid—were all dead of the bomb concussion and falling debris." Sampson shook his head.

"If you'd left then, you'd have been safe," I reminded him.

"Yes, but..." He sighed. "The bomb had knocked over a small chest and all this gold, all these diamonds, were spilling out onto the floor. I had my doctor's bag. I only took a handful."

"Of each." I was pushing him now.

He sighed. "Of each. I hid everything down in the bottom of my bag and started to leave to report their deaths when the building came down." He looked at each of us in turn. "They had no family left. Their gold and jewels just went to the government, if it wasn't all stolen. I told the rescuers I had gone in and found everyone dead. The rescuers took me to the hospital without looking inside my bag. That was how I could afford to buy this practice from Forrester's daughter."

"And Mrs. Bryant had no idea," I said.

"No one did. Please don't tell," the doctor begged us, looking from one to the other.

Chapter Seventeen

"Looting a bombed-out house is a crime. I have to tell the inspector," Bell said.

"Of course. Just no one else," Sampson said, sounding worried.

"No, this village needs a doctor, and if they knew you were a thief, they would have nothing else to do with you, while you would end up in jail. It serves no purpose to spread this story around, as long as you didn't kill Mrs. Bryant or Mrs. Withins." I watched Sampson as I spoke.

"I wouldn't kill anyone, and I wasn't being blackmailed."

"Which one of your patients was?" I asked.

"I don't know. I am angry about the idea that my medical notes could be used to blackmail my patients." Now he just sounded furious as he spit out the words.

"Yet someone killed Mrs. Bryant because of it," I snapped back at him. "You need to open your records to the inspector to find this third blackmail victim."

"No."

"Then be prepared to learn how people in this village react to having a thief in their midst." I crossed my arms and stared at him.

His eyes widened. "You wouldn't. You couldn't. You promised."

"That was before you told me you would allow a killer to walk free among us." I wouldn't do it, but I really wanted to convince the doctor to let us look in the files.

He slammed his fist on the table next to him. "Fine. See what you can uncover. There's nothing there."

"Let's start with Mrs. Henrietta Johnson and her children."

We went into the surgery office and Dr. Sampson found Mrs. Johnson's records under "Deceased" and her children under the regular files. Bell and I started reading, passing the records back and forth.

Henrietta Johnson had been in her sixties and suffered from heart disease due to high blood pressure. Her body was found on the bank of the Wenmire Brook along a stony patch. It was early in the morning and there were no witnesses to her fall. The most likely cause was tripping accidentally or because of dizziness brought on by high blood pressure, causing a head injury. The second most likely cause was a push, but there was no evidence because she wore a heavy coat that would have blocked any bruises left by a push and there were no witnesses.

"You examined the body?" I asked.

"Yes, before she went to the coroner. Neither of us found anything that pointed to foul play."

"Then why mention it?" That made no sense to me.

"Because the younger daughter, Mrs. Norris, believed the older daughter, Mrs. Sharp, had caused her death and was saying so to anyone who would listen."

"She was. She was driving us all crazy," Bell added.

"And this was because Mrs. Sharp wanted her sister to help out at their mother's house, I think you told me," I said.

"There were chickens and a large garden to care for and Mrs. Johnson couldn't manage it on her own. Mrs. Sharp and her children were doing as much as they could, the children living at a distance, so she asked Mrs. Norris and her children who lived nearby to help out," Bell explained.

"It sounds reasonable."

"To you and me, maybe," Bell said. "Mrs. Norris said absolutely not. Her daughter has her schoolwork, her son has a dodgy ticker, and she didn't have the time. So, Mrs. Sharp says, 'It doesn't stop you from taking the vegetables and the eggs, does it?'"

"Starting a family feud that continues. Somehow, the son managed to stay out of it," Dr. Sampson told us.

"Mrs. Norris's son?" I asked.

"No," Dr. Sampson said. "Mrs. Johnson's son Tom. He and his wife Rose have a farm outside of town, and both of them helped Mrs. Sharp with his mother's garden without fighting with the other sister, Mrs. Norris."

"Frankly, I think Mrs. Norris coddles that son of hers a bit," Sampson continued, sounding annoyed. "He travels into Oxford a couple of times a week by bus to work in an office. And he does this without any difficulty. But the army somehow decided his heart was damaged enough they don't even want him working in one of their offices here in the manor house."

"Do you have records on him from Dr. Forrester?" I asked.

"I'm sure I do somewhere, but I've only seen him once. His mother thought Dr. Forrester was more thorough with her son's care, and so she left this practice to go to one in Oxford, a Dr. Embleton. Her right, of course."

I began to look through Dr. Forrester's records, finally finding them filed under "J." Benjamin Norris didn't have a particularly thick file until 1937, when his mother began bringing him in nearly weekly.

Reading through the file, it seemed the boy had a normal, healthy childhood, except he had a touch of bronchitis. Then a few years before, he began to have asthmatic episodes, particularly in prolonged wet spells. I didn't see anywhere that his heart was mentioned.

I showed Dr. Sampson the file on the Norris boy that Dr. Forrester had compiled. "May we see your files on the Norris family?" I asked.

"Those files are over there in that cabinet. It's where I

put the files of patients who have left the practice."

They were in no particular order, so it was a bit more of a challenge.

But I found the Norris records without much effort, since there were few patients who had left Dr. Sampson. I suspected most people had the same reaction I had. He was a good doctor.

Sampson had used a great deal of abbreviations and quotes in his notes on Benjamin Norris. *He exhibited a small degree of wheezing. Mother states he has lng. stnd. hrt. cond. No evidence.* This was followed by half a page of notes from what must have been a lengthy and thorough examination.

Mother states needs complete exemp. from military svc. Sugg. office or rear lines work suit.

The notes ended with *"Mother states they will not be coming back here."*

I handed the files to the doctor. "What do you make of all this?"

The doctor started reading his own notes. "I remember her," he said.

"You did a thorough examination on his heart, or at least that's how it read to me. Why was she so certain he had a long-standing heart condition and then say they weren't coming back to your practice?"

"First-time mothers are frequently overcautious. You've been through that yourself, but as you develop more experience with your son, you develop an understanding of what is normal and what is not. Not all mothers have as much sense as you. Especially widows. No matter how many children they have, they are particularly cautious about the health of their firstborn son."

"What happened to Mr. Norris?"

"A sad story. It's in Dr. Forrester's notes. This was perhaps in the mid-1930s. Mr. Norris got a cut on his foot. It became infected. There was nothing they could do. Even amputation didn't stop the infection, and he died about a week later. It was after that Mrs. Norris became over-solicitous about Benjamin's health," Dr. Sampson told us.

"Now, please read Dr. Forrester's notes on young Benjamin," I said.

Dr. Sampson read through quickly and then went back and went over the notes again with more interest. "I wonder where she got the idea he has serious heart issues?"

"From another doctor?" Bell suggested.

"That's entirely possible. She seemed pretty upset when she brought Benjamin into my surgery."

"But he's been declared exempt from conscription, hasn't he?" I asked.

"That's what I've heard around the village. His asthma might have made him ineligible for military service, but I imagine he could serve as a clerk in an office, or a cook or a mechanic. Perhaps his mother is trying to get him a position in the office she works in at the manor house. In the meantime, he can continue his work at the Oxford town hall. These things take time," the doctor said.

"Then whatever Mrs. Bryant found in Mrs. Johnson's records or Benjamin Norris's, there is nothing there for her to blackmail Mrs. Norris or Mrs. Sharp." I sat down dejectedly.

"Exactly. I think you need to look elsewhere for your third blackmail victim," Dr. Sampson said.

"Was there anything else odd about someone's medical records? That's where you found Mrs. Bryant looking for people to blackmail, or at least that's how it appears."

"Mrs. Redmond, Mrs. Bryant was caught searching through my medical files on two occasions that I know of, and it is believed she used the information to blackmail people, but that doesn't mean this third victim, this killer, came to her attention through my medical records."

I thought about it before I nodded. "That's fair enough. But where else could Mrs. Bryant learn other people's secrets?"

"The WI?" the doctor suggested drily.

Bell burst out laughing. "Admit it, Mrs. Redmond. You ladies enjoy your WI meetings, but they frighten the men in the village."

"Why?" I wasn't certain if I was more indignant or curious.

"Because of all the gossip, and opportunities for the wrong thing to be said, and comparing notes. Heaven help anyone with a secret they want to hide if there's a WI meeting in the area."

"There is one this week. I'll have to keep my ears open for anything Mrs. Bryant may have heard." But how would I do this?

* * *

I waited until the morning of the WI meeting before I said anything to Esther. "Who did Mrs. Bryant talk to or about at her last WI meeting?"

"Still trying to figure out who killed her?"

"Yes. On one level, this village hasn't changed, but if you look deeper, you'll see it's not as friendly, nor as trusting, as it was before she died."

Esther thought about it for a minute. "You're right. We've all been on edge and watching the others in the village out of the corners of our eyes. Let's see. I know she was speaking to Mrs. Otterfield, but she's the chair and Mrs. Bryant was the secretary. She spoke to Lady Agatha when she first came in, but that would have been good manners."

Her two long-time victims. "Can you think of anyone else?"

"Let me mull this over in my mind while we go up there."

We got ready and walked up to the community hall, Stevie in his pram looking all around him as he rolled halfway over. We reached the double front doors the same time as Lady Agatha, Lady Lydia, and Jane and Andrew, or Lady Jane and Lord Andrew, if I was being correct.

"Do you want to take the boys on a walk before lunch?" I asked Jane.

"Perfect," she replied.

Walking from the bright sunshine to the relative darkness of the hall left me temporarily blind. I plowed into a woman with Stevie's pram and apologized, having no idea who I was apologizing to.

"Here, I'll get out of the way and you go ahead," a woman's voice said, sounding a little annoyed.

"Thank you. I'm so sorry. I came in from the sunlight and couldn't see anything." By then, my eyes had adjusted. "Oh, Mrs. Sharp. I am so sorry."

"I'm fine. Really." She walked to the side of the hall, away from me.

Jane signaled me to join her and Andrew near the back of the hall and on the other side. Esther headed over to join the primary school mothers. I followed Jane.

"Do you remember who Mrs. Bryant talked to at her last WI meeting before she was murdered?"

"Still trying to find her killer?" Jane asked.

"I don't enjoy living in a village with a murderer."

"None of us do. And you think it was someone she spoke to here?"

"Possibly. It was the last public meeting in the village before she died," I said.

"And she was dead just a couple of days later. Have you

talked to Elfrieda?"

"Why would I talk to Elfrieda?" The jump in subject matter confused me.

"After the meeting, Mrs. Bryant called to Elfrieda to talk to her as they walked down the lane. Both their houses were in that direction."

"Any idea what they talked about?"

"Whatever Mrs. Bryant said made Elfrieda furious. You've seen her. She's big and strong and she got right in front of Mrs. Bryant, stood up to her, and told her off. Then Elfrieda walked off and Mrs. Bryant stood there looking shocked." Jane smiled. "It was as if Elfrieda had told a two-year-old no for the first time."

"Any idea what it could have been about?" I asked, letting my interest show.

"I think Elfrieda has a boyfriend. A big, slow farmhand named Zeke who's missing part of his right hand. A little old for conscription at the moment, but the hand guarantees he won't be called up. No trigger finger, and the MOD wouldn't want him for anything else. He would be Elfrieda's first boyfriend, I think. Mrs. Bryant might have been teasing her about it. Elfrieda wouldn't find it amusing."

"Or she might have been trying a little blackmail."

"You'd need a subtler mind than Elfrieda's to try blackmail on." Jane looked at me and shrugged, then glanced at the stage. "They're ready to start."

We sat our sons on our laps and listened to the meeting.

There were reminders about where to take old newspapers, tin foil, and damaged pots and pans for salvage. A report that the Mothers' Guild planned to have a school uniform swap in the hall shortly before the start of term in the autumn. And then the main program, Peggy Norris speaking on helping the older citizens of the village around their homes and gardens while sons and grandsons were away in the military.

As soon as Frances Otterfield announced the speaker and subject, Patricia Sharp picked up her gloves and bag and marched out of the hall. A number of women exchanged looks as her heels clicked on the wooden floor.

"You know about the feud between Patricia and her sister, Peggy Norris?" Jane asked.

"Yes. That topic seems rather insensitive," I replied.

Another baby's mother, who had joined us after the meeting started, said, "That's exactly the subject they quarreled about. You know their mother, Mrs. Johnson, was out on the path along the Wenmire that morning taking a shortcut to her neighbors, the Shorts, most likely in an effort to find somebody to help her light her stove. She'd dropped and broken her glasses and couldn't see to do anything."

"Is this the sort of thing the sisters were fighting about?" I asked. And then I realized, I thought I knew how Mrs. Johnson died.

Chapter Eighteen

"Did Mrs. Johnson wear her glasses all the time?" I asked.

"Yes, of course," the baby's mother told me. "She was blind as a bat without them." Jane nodded.

"But how do you know where she was going and that her glasses were already broken?"

"That's easy," the woman told me. "Peggy found her broken spectacles when she went through her mother's cottage a day or two after she died. Mrs. Johnson went to the Shorts for help the last time she broke her glasses to see if they could light her stove fire in the morning since she couldn't. She couldn't ask Patricia to take her to get her glasses fixed until she returned from London."

"I need to talk to Dr. Sampson and Constable Bell." I shot a frustrated glance at my son and immediately felt guilty. I couldn't leave my baby, at least not until I could hand him off to Esther.

In the meantime, Peggy Norris was going on about helping the old dears, which caused more than a few raised eyebrows.

"Where can someone get eyeglasses and lenses repaired or replaced?"

"Oxford," Jane told me. "Lydia took Agatha in to get hers repaired a couple of weeks ago."

"And how do you get there?"

"By the bus." The baby's mother sounded as if she couldn't believe how ignorant I was.

"Mrs. Johnson would have needed someone to take her by bus and to find the optician once they arrived in Oxford, wouldn't she?" I was half thinking aloud.

"And this happened when Mrs. Sharp was in London with the WI. She might not have known about her mother's eyeglasses," Jane said.

"But if anyone knew, they would have told Mrs. Norris, knowing Mrs. Sharp was out of town," the baby's mother said, filling in the blanks for us.

"Did the Shorts know that Mrs. Johnson was coming over looking for help that day?" I asked.

"No, but Mrs. Short said they'd have gladly started the stove. They were fond of the old woman."

"When was the last time Mrs. Norris spoke to her mother?"

"Days before she died. No one had seen her in the area of her mother's cottage for nearly a week. Not after the fight she and her sister had."

I decided this baby's mother was full of information. I hoped she never wanted to gossip about me. "Mrs. Norris knew about the WI trip to London Mrs. Sharp was going on?"

"That was part of the argument."

"Did you hear it?" With any luck, she had.

"Yes. I was walking the older three children back from the village school and pushing the baby in her pram when we passed Mrs. Norris and Mrs. Sharp in the lane. They weren't making any effort to keep their voices down."

Neither was the baby's mother. We were getting a few dirty looks from the rows of women in front of us, but Peggy Norris didn't seem to be paying us any attention. I suspected she either loved the sound of her own voice or she was so nervous about public speaking she was unaware of anything else going on in the hall.

"Mrs. Sharp said she thought if Rose Johnson, Tom's wife, could help and not take any of their mother's garden produce, that Mrs. Norris could be kind enough to help out when she took the produce. Mrs. Norris said Rose has a whole farm full of produce to feed her family while she, Mrs. Norris, had two children to feed. Mrs. Sharp said then her children could help if they wanted to eat. Everyone else did." The baby's mother nodded vigorously at that.

Peggy Norris finished her talk, smiled at us all, and left the podium.

"Finally," someone near us murmured.

Shortly thereafter, the meeting came to a close and we all began to gather our things. I thanked the infant's mother and Jane for their help as I snatched up my purse, pulled on my gloves, and headed out the door.

I was halfway to the constabulary house before Esther came out of the hall and looked around for me. I waved to her and kept on, walking into the building without knocking.

Both Constable Bell and Inspector Grimsby were seated around the desk, and Grimsby rose to help me inside with the pram.

"Did you know about Mrs. Johnson's glasses?" I asked before I was the whole way inside the building.

They both looked at me blankly.

"Apparently, Mrs. Johnson had broken her glasses and couldn't see to start the fire in her stove. That's why she hadn't started it. She was walking over to her neighbors, the Shorts, to ask them to light the fire when she fell. Wouldn't Mrs. Bryant have had a great time blackmailing Peggy Norris over that? I just sat through a painfully long talk by her on taking care of our elders, and she wasn't doing anything for her own mother. She hadn't been to see her in almost a week."

"Did this come out at the inquest?" Grimsby asked.

"About the glasses? No. That gives more credence to Mrs. Johnson's death being accidental, but hardly explains why her daughter was blaming her sister for killing their mother," Constable Bell said.

"To draw our attention away from her?" the inspector said, raising his brows.

Bell shook his head. "How does this help us with Mrs. Bryant's murder? Hadn't she already begun to collect blackmail payments from the third victim before Mrs. Johnson died?"

"She had," Grimsby agreed.

"Unless Mrs. Bryant had learned something that Mrs. Norris had done before her mother died. Maybe Mrs. Norris stole from her mother, or maybe nothing that has anything to do with her mother."

"But what if it didn't have anything to do with her mother?" Bell asked.

I dropped into a free chair. "I don't know. Mrs. Bryant's first two blackmail victims were found by going through Dr. Forrester's records. Our best guess for finding the third victim was something in Dr. Sampson's records before he fired her."

"And the only death that seemed suspicious in that time frame was Mrs. Johnson's," Grimsby said. "But what if it wasn't a death. What if the patient recovered?"

"That means talking to Dr. Sampson again to see if anyone recovered, giving his or her relatives a shock." I looked from Grimsby to Bell.

"Or someone took ill doing something they shouldn't," Bell suggested.

"Another question for Dr. Sampson," Grimsby agreed.

"What about anyone with an illness or injury that Dr. Sampson questioned in his own mind but didn't say anything about? Whether or not he put his questions into his notes," I added.

"If he didn't put it into his notes, how would Mrs. Bryant know?" Bell asked.

"Because maybe she had the same questions Dr. Sampson had."

"How could she? She's not a doctor."

"But she was in the office. She could have overheard something. Dr. Sampson asked the patient a question and Mrs. Bryant knew the answer wasn't the truth. That would have made her ask questions of other people or the patient until she had something she could blackmail someone with. Or failing that, gossip about."

"We don't know she started any of her blackmail schemes by reading the medical records. They're hard to read. She might have begun by listening at keyholes," Grimsby said. "You knew her, Bell. Was she the type to listen at keyholes?"

"Keyholes, shops, out in the street, anywhere people gathered. She enjoyed listening and she enjoyed spreading malicious gossip. It would have been hard for her to keep her mouth shut long enough to blackmail anybody." Bell shook his head.

"She only had three blackmail victims in all those years. Suppose these were the three best stories, or the three best tales for which someone would give her money over a long period."

"You want me to get Dr. Sampson to relay any good tales from his time here and then check to see if any of these could have made their way into gossip." Grimsby studied me.

"Yes," I replied. "I believe Dr. Sampson knows the secret someone was hiding that led to Mrs. Bryant's death. He just doesn't know he knows."

"You mean, something similar to Bud's poisoning," the constable said.

Grimsby and I stared at him. "You mentioned that before. What happened?" I asked.

"Bud will eat vegetable stew, Woolton pie, anything as long as it has enough onions in it."

"How did he get poisoned?" Grimsby asked, sounding annoyed that Bell wasn't coming to the point.

"Brenda, his wife, had run out of onions, but someone told her where they were growing wild in an abandoned field by the stream. She went and collected some, chopped them up, and put them in the Woolton pie. Bud was feeling peckish and had an early dinner. He was sick before anyone else had any."

"So, his wife made a mistake. Big deal," Grimsby said. "Wild onions aren't to everyone's taste."

"It was autumn crocus—you can't eat them. He was lucky to survive. Dr. Sampson didn't think he was going to for a day or two. And then there would have to have been an inquest." Bell smiled then. "But he lived, so it was all good."

"I think I'll have another talk with the doctor," Grimsby said.

Agreeing that was a good idea, I left the constabulary house, pushing Stevie toward home in the bright sunshine. I was ready for my luncheon and I was sure he was, too. Halfway there, I ran into Mr. MacDonald.

"You've been to the constabulary house, have you?" he asked. "Any further along?"

"Constable Bell came up with another possibility." I told him about the poisoning at the pub.

"Are they still together?"

"I think so."

"Then I'm sure it was just an accident. You'll have to keep looking." And with a cheery wave, Mr. MacDonald was off.

I fed Stevie first and put him down for a nap before I joined Esther in the dining room. "Anything left?"

"Of course," she told me. "And we've been invited to tea at the lodge by Lady Agatha."

"Why?"

"After the meeting, we stood outside and talked for a little while about how unsafe we feel with two murders in the village. We're going to talk about steps we can take to make the village safer."

"Don't try to blackmail your neighbors. One of them is very upset by the idea." My words sounded sarcastic, but as I put vegetables on my plate and took a slice of bread, I realized it was also true.

"Was Mrs. Withins a blackmailer?" Esther asked.

"I don't know. It may have been that she saw activity in her neighbor's house and went over to investigate, not realizing it was the killer returning to the scene of the crime to retrieve what she hadn't found the first time."

"Is what she wanted still there?"

"No." I had to be honest with Esther.

"How can you be so sure?" Esther poured herself another glass of water.

"Because I found it and turned it into the police." I quickly took another bite before she thought of any more questions to ask and stop me from eating. It had been a long time since breakfast.

"They're having tea at five. Please come with me."

"Of course. What about Stevie?"

"Nanny Goldie will watch the children." Then Esther gave me a grin. "The way you are eating, you need to help me weed when you are finished."

"Glad to know I'm good for something." I smiled in return and hurried to finish my meal.

By five o'clock, we had weeded a sizable section of the vegetable garden and cleaned up to make ourselves presentable at the lodge. I wasn't surprised that we weren't the only guests.

Of course, Mrs. Brown-Dunn and Frances Otterfield were there, because Lady Agatha needed her remaining acolyte present and Mrs. Otterfield and Lady Lydia reinforced each other's snobbery as no one else would. A number of women from the village I expected to see weren't there because they held down jobs that kept them away or were farmers' wives who had chores around the farm to take care of.

Elfrieda was there along with Sally, the baker, and Brenda, the pub landlord's wife, since they worked different hours than the women who worked in the offices and shops. I couldn't look Brenda in the eye, not with the story I'd heard earlier that day.

Esther and I greeted Elfrieda as we walked inside the grand front entrance of the lodge. I wondered just how grand the entrance to the manor house was, if the lodge was anything to go by.

We took seats in the large drawing room, which were arranged to more or less face the large chair set in front of the cold fireplace. Lady Agatha took her place in that seat as I was certain she would, with Lady Lydia, Jane, Mrs. Brown-Dunn, and Mrs. Otterfield seated in what represented the first row by a couple of chairs on either side of a central aisle.

Esther, a few other ladies, and I took the second row, with the rest in the third.

"We'll break for tea in a few minutes," Lady Agatha

began in her low aristocratic tone, "but first, I would appreciate it if we could discuss what we can do to protect ourselves from this killer in our village. Anyone?"

I kept very quiet, hoping no one would look at me. No such luck. Everyone was staring at me.

"Mrs. Redmond, you were first on the scene of both murders. What do you think we can do to protect ourselves?" Lady Agatha said as if prodding a reluctant serf.

I gave her a fake smile and said, "As I told Esther at luncheon, the best way to keep safe is to not blackmail your neighbors."

More than one lady made a choking sound.

"Not blackmail…? Surely, Mrs. Redmond…" Lady Agatha said. "Mrs. Withins would never…"

"Mrs. Bryant was a blackmailer, as the police have established. Mrs. Withins had either decided to take over Mrs. Bryant's role, or she was watching through her lace curtains and saw the murderer return to the scene of the crime. Instead of calling the police, she decided to investigate on her own. Neither plan was a safe one."

"None of us would dream of blackmailing our friends and neighbors," Lady Lydia shrieked, clutching at the silk scarf around her shoulders.

"Mrs. Bryant apparently did, and it led to her murder. I'd avoid sending threatening letters right now, because you might inadvertently send one to the killer. Someone has a secret that they've killed to keep anyone from learning."

A voice from behind me said, "God help anyone with anything to hide."

I recognized Elfrieda's voice and decided she was more astute than I had thought.

Chapter Nineteen

"No, Elfrieda, I wouldn't say that. If everyone just refrains from gossip, it should go a long way to protect all of us from murder." I glanced around at the ladies in the room.

Mrs. Brown-Dunn shook her gray curls. "Are you saying that the only way to find the killer is to find out all the secrets in the village? Isn't that what you've been doing for the police?" She looked straight at me.

I felt the heat rising up my cheeks. "They've been using me as a photographer. Anyone who's tried to tell me anything, I've suggested they tell Inspector Grimsby. He's very easy to talk to."

"But we've known each other's secrets for ages. Why

would anyone blackmail or kill someone now?" Sally, the baker, declared through pale, puffy cheeks that reminded me of gigantic, unbaked muffins.

"How many people have lived in this village for twenty years?" I asked. A few hands went up, including the baker.

"Ten years?" A few more were raised.

"Most of us, myself included, are relative newcomers to the village." Before I could go any further, Mrs. Brown-Dunn broke in.

"But a lot of the newcomers married farmers on the edge of the village or have taken over shops when the old owners died off. Such as our doctor. Or the government sent here to work in the manor house." She looked at me pointedly and continued, "That leaves us with a small group who are new to the village and its secrets, and there's where you'll find your killer."

"Unless a long-time resident has a new secret, giving new fodder to the blackmailer," Jane said.

It dawned on me that there was another question I should ask. "But wait. Has anyone received a blackmail letter since Mrs. Bryant died?" I asked.

Everyone shook their heads, puzzled and unsure about their friends.

"How about a poisoned pen letter?" I continued.

Everyone indicated negative.

"Has anyone come into money recently?" Mrs. Brown-Dunn asked.

Again, everyone shook their heads.

"Who here enjoyed sharing gossip with Mrs. Bryant?" Mrs. Brown-Dunn asked, peering around the room and then at me.

Everyone leaned back in their seats away from her.

Mrs. Brown-Dunn was asking good questions, except she kept staring at me as she asked them. It was obvious she was convinced I was the killer.

"I think," Lady Agatha said, taking charge of the meeting before someone had to break up a fight, "we should agree among ourselves to go everywhere in pairs."

"Should we assign partners?" Lady Lydia asked, sounding a little too eager to perform that task.

"I don't think that's necessary. Just a request to a family member or neighbor should do the trick. Any other suggestions?"

When no one responded, Lady Lydia said, "I think, Lady Agatha, it's time for tea."

Lady Agatha led the way, followed by Mrs. Brown-Dunn, Mrs. Otterfield, and then Brenda, the publican's wife. Esther and I waited for Jane to bring up the rear. I wanted to keep my distance until Inspector Grimsby had his chance to ask his questions.

"Shouldn't you...?" I asked Jane, knowing she was the mother of the current earl.

She gave me a frantic look. "Goodness, no. Please. That just starts more sniping." She looked around for another subject and said, "Esther said your husband will have leave soon. Is he coming here?"

"Yes, which will cause my father to appear more often. To hear my father, Stevie is his and Adam's child, and I am just a servant."

"That must be uncomfortable," Sally, the baker said. Her pale cheeks were pudgy, an unhealthy doughiness with two raisin-colored eyes sunk deep inside. I had noticed her two young children had the same raised-dough look about them, making me wonder at their diet.

"But it would be more uncomfortable for your father or Adam if one of them had to give birth," Elfrieda said with a raucous laugh.

Everyone turned to look at her, but this didn't seem to bother her at all as she took another tiny sandwich and plopped it in her mouth.

"Mrs. Redmond, do you really think if we just mind our own business that we won't disturb the killer and he'll leave us alone?" one of the older village ladies asked.

"Yes, but remember, from what we've learned, the killer is probably a woman."

"How dreadful." The old woman set down her teacup and fluttered her hands.

I walked over to her. "Now, I know you're not a gossip and you're not a blackmailer, so you have nothing to worry about."

"I hope you're right, young lady," she said to me. "Are

the police making any progress?"

"They aren't telling me, whatever they are doing."

"I still think it's someone from outside the village, brought in to work in the manor house," one of the women near the front of the line said. "That Mr. MacDonald, for instance. He pops up all over the village."

"I've seen him hanging around the Old Vicarage," someone else said. I blinked as I glanced at Esther. The Old Vicarage was the name of her home. "Is he a special friend of yours, Mrs. Redmond?"

"What? No." I tried to guess who had asked that question, but there were several women between the speaker and me.

"Then how did you get mixed up with the police?" someone else asked.

"My husband bought me a really nice camera to take pictures of our son to send to him. As a reporter on a London newspaper, I've been at crime scenes where I've seen some of the tasks the forensics officers carry out. When Constable Bell found Mrs. Bryant, he came looking for Dr. Sampson, who was checking out my Stevie. The constable seemed unsure of himself so I offered to help. By taking the crime scene photographs," I quickly added.

"Could you take a photo of my children to send to their father?" Sally the baker asked. "I'd pay you for the developing."

And in an instant the worry over being murdered

disappeared to be replaced by talk of mail deliveries and photographs. And then talk went around, as it did, to the newest two men to move into billets in our village. Mrs. Bryant's cottage was being put to use for two of the older men working at the manor house for the Ministry of Defense, and the guess was that next Mrs. Withins's house would be used to billet MOD workers, as soon as her daughter finished clearing it out.

"I told them as long as I've got Mr. MacDonald to do for, I'll cook and clean for the men at Mrs. Bryant's house too," Mrs. Coffey told us. "I've not heard who will be doing for anyone who moves into Mrs. Withins's."

"Who knows how long it will take that girl to shift a few items out of her mother's house? She'll have to leave the bed linens and pots and pans and plates," Mrs. Brown-Dunn said.

"No worries there," someone told her. "The MOD is sending someone around with boxes and help and they'll have her out the door in a jiffy. They need more room for workers at the manor house."

I glanced at Jane, who shrugged. "At least no one is talking about setting up patrols around the village."

"Oh, they wouldn't." My murmur sounded horrified to my own ears.

"Carry it out? No, but I could see them talk about it until dinnertime."

We finished our tea and drifted away, thanking Lady

Agatha for the invitation. Esther and I reached home in time to see to the children's dinner, which included mashed potatoes and smushed peas for Stevie. He was beginning to take to the idea of eating mushy food. In another month, I expected him to want to use Esther's old highchair.

Then it was bath time and bedtime. Stevie settled down quickly, as he always did, but Esther's children had reached the age where they needed to be read a few stories before they would settle down. The longer daylight in the evenings as the nights grew shorter didn't help convince them to go to sleep.

We waited dinner until Esther was finished with the nighttime ritual and could come downstairs. Magda was good at guessing what time the children would finally settle down in their beds, and she brought out supper, vegetables from the garden and baked fish, the moment Esther's feet reached the ground floor.

Nanny Goldie, who seemed to be the nervous sort when dealing with the adults in the village, while the children didn't faze her in the least, asked about the meeting at the "grand ladies'" house.

"The only idea of any merit was to travel the village in groups of two," Esther said.

"And if you haven't tried to blackmail anyone, you should have nothing to worry about," I added.

"How could I blackmail anyone?" she asked. "I don't know anyone's secrets."

"So you say," I said to tease her, but she only looked frightened and set down her fork.

"Don't tease her, Livvy," Esther said.

"I'm sorry, Goldie. I was teasing you, but you didn't understand the joke. Please accept my apologies." I watched her for a moment before she nodded. "Thank you. I'll try to keep my jokes to myself, unless it is something you'll understand."

She nodded again and continued eating.

"And really, both of you, Magda and Goldie, you have nothing to worry about. We know Mrs. Bryant was a blackmailer. We think Mrs. Withins either planned to take over from her or saw someone in her neighbor's house and investigated. But the important fact was both women lived alone."

"Mrs. Bryant had a lodger in—Mr. MacDonald, working at the manor house," Esther reminded me.

"Who worked very long hours and was seldom at her house," I countered.

"Neither of you have involved yourselves with the life of the village," Esther said. "Unlike Livvy who has stuck her nose in both murders as well as the police investigation. If the killer wants to get anyone, it will be Livvy."

"Thanks," I said, staring at Esther. "This wasn't something I had planned to do."

"I know. My father says you have a nose for it. Or you attract trouble. He says that's what makes you a good reporter."

"Now you're scaring both Nanny Goldie and me," I told her.

"I will stay far away from you," Nanny said.

"Great," I murmured and focused on my dinner.

* * *

The letter I'd been waiting for from Adam arrived with the first post the next morning. I set Stevie down in his pram and ripped open the letter. I scanned it quickly and then shouted, "Adam will be here for nearly two weeks starting Friday."

Either my shouting or my jumping up and down frightened Stevie and he wailed and shook his fists and feet. I picked him up and said, "You're going to love seeing your papa again. I'm going to love seeing your papa again."

Esther and Goldie hugged me and Magda shouted her enthusiasm from the kitchen.

"I want to tell everyone, but that wouldn't be too tactful, with Lady Lydia and Jane's losses. That's something else Hitler has stolen from us, the ability to be truly, gloriously happy because so many have already lost so much."

"Even if it wouldn't be tactful to shout in the green now, I'm sure everyone will be truly happy to meet him while he's here. We wish the best for all our soldiers and sailors, no matter what we've lost as individuals," Esther told me.

Nothing would ruin my mood that morning. I hummed

nursery rhymes as I hauled the laundry to Elfrieda. I hummed Christmas carols as I weeded the garden. Mr. MacDonald, taking a walk around the green as he enjoyed doing every day before lunch, looked over the fence around the side garden where I was weeding and said, "Someone is in a happy frame of mind today."

Glad of an excuse to stand up straight, I rose and walked over to the fence. "My husband is getting two weeks' leave before he gets transferred. He'll be here Friday."

"Do you know where he's getting transferred?"

"Of course not, but based on where he was sent before the Blitz, someplace overseas and dangerous." I took a deep breath. "And how are you, Mr. MacDonald? Settling in all right at Mrs. Coffey's?"

"Of course. You've never seen the manor house, have you?"

"No. I've seen the lodge at the end of the drive and it is gorgeous. You must have a beautiful background for your typewriter."

He laughed. "I do. The interior is Georgian and quite splendid. Carved ceilings and magnificent staircases."

"It's too bad you have to work so hard. That everyone has to work so hard these days. Still, you have a lovely place to spend your days."

Mr. MacDonald turned serious. "You're worried about what your husband will be surrounded with, aren't you?"

I nodded, biting my lip to fight back tears. I hadn't

admitted to myself until now how frightened I was about where they would be sending Adam once this two weeks' leave was over. I took a deep, ragged breath and gained mastery of myself. "Doesn't do any good to worry, does it?"

"No." He shook his head and then gave me a smile. "I wish everyone had your outlook."

"If everyone had my view, Hitler would be struck by a lightning bolt and the war would be over."

"That is fervently to be wished for. Well, I must get on." With a pat on my hand resting on the fence and an encouraging smile, he walked off around the green in his usual pattern.

"Horrid man."

I glanced over to see Peggy Norris coming toward the fence. "What's wrong?"

"MacDonald. No one is safe once he gets his talons into you."

"Golly. Not another blackmailer." I seemed to have them on the brain.

"No." She looked shocked and shook her head. "Just problems within the various offices of the MOD."

"I wouldn't know about that, since I never worked for them." Not quite a lie. I didn't think Sir Malcolm was MOD, although he qualified as a horrid man. Who did our spymaster work for? Probably MI something.

"I'm sure it's the same in every office, though, isn't it?" she said.

"Probably," I agreed. "It could be that way at the newspaper I worked for." I watched her walk away to cook lunch for her children while I thought, there went a woman who was never going to suffer from this war the way the rest of us did because her husband was dead and her son wouldn't be sent away to the military or would only have a desk job the same as Mr. MacDonald.

I felt a genuine dislike for Peggy Norris.

Chapter Twenty

I don't remember any details about Adam's first day or two in Chipping Ford, because all I was aware of was that Adam was here. In the same room or the same building with me. I could see him, hear his voice, touch him. I had to keep a hand on him all the time, touching his shoulder or holding his hand, while he was constantly touching Stevie or me. I suppose we ate because Magda would have seen to it, but I don't remember a single dish. I suppose we slept, but I only remember listening to Stevie's baby noises while I kept a hand on Adam, not wanting to let him go.

Then Sunday happened with all its frustrations, starting with my father.

We'd barely had time to get cleaned up and dressed when Sir Henry and my father pulled up out front of Esther's large cottage. And then a third party climbed out of the back seat of Sir Henry's automobile—James Powell. Both he and Adam were in uniform, so we stood out when we walked into church for Sunday service.

"How did you manage it?" Esther asked James.

"I don't have to work until tonight, and your father said he was driving up and would be back in London before I was due back, so I hitched a ride with him."

"I'm glad you did," Esther responded.

There were a few other uniforms in the congregation, men and women who worked at the manor house, but most of us were in dowdy civilian dress. The vicar, tipped off by someone, called for special blessings for those who would be going overseas to continue the fight, and I pressed Adam's hand extra hard. We sang the hymns loudly if not completely in tune, for which I blamed the organ.

Inspector Grimsby and Constable Bell slid in the back of the church during the second hymn, allowing all of us to glance back and see who had entered. Grimsby caught my eye and nodded.

"Not this week or next," I thought. I was willing to chase down clues and read medical records in our hunt for a killer, but not while Adam was in the village. He was leaving Friday morning next week. I'd help again after that.

"Who is that?" Adam asked, seeing the look Grimsby gave me.

"A police inspector."

"The one you've been working with since you came here?" Adam's look was sharp.

"I'll deal with him after your leave ends." I put my arm

around Adam's and leaned in.

"If you don't, I will." Adam sounded firm, serious, and a little stubborn.

"I'll deal with him."

My father, on my other side, heard the last part of our conversation and said, "Olivia. Now is not the time."

Both Adam and I gave him a piercing look.

The sermon was on "Love Thy Neighbor," which included not blackmailing them or gossiping about them, and certainly not murdering a fellow villager. It was tedious enough that if I were the killer, I would have confessed just to make the vicar stop.

Finally, the last hymn wound down with the recessional and we were all free to escape.

As soon as we stepped out into the churchyard, several people from the MOD at the manor house and the leaders of local society, starting with Lady Agatha, all had to shake Adam's hand and wish him luck. While he was occupied balancing on his crutches with all the attention, and my father was talking to Sir Henry, I stepped aside to talk to Grimsby and Bell.

"I came here today to let you know I'm headed back to Oxford. There are cases there we can make some progress on. But I see you're otherwise occupied and won't miss my help," Grimsby said.

"Adam is here until Friday morning next week. If you need me after that, you have only to ask, but only after," I told him.

"Keep your ears open," Bell said, "and I will, too."

I nodded my agreement and slipped next to Adam again.

Mr. MacDonald came up to us and put out his hand to Adam. "Welcome to Chipping Ford, Major Redmond. I know you've been sorely missed." He introduced himself and they shook hands.

"You're not part of the police service, are you?" Adam asked.

"No, I work for the MOD at the manor house. You've heard about our murders? Oh, you would have heard because your camera has been such a help to the police, as has Mrs. Redmond."

Adam looked at me. "I'll tell you later," I said and smiled.

Mr. MacDonald said, "If you'll excuse me, I need to say a few words to the inspector before he goes back to Oxford. See all three of you around the village." With a jaunty wave, he walked across the churchyard to where Grimsby and Bell were standing.

"How did he know the inspector is going back to Oxford?" I asked myself. I didn't have time to speculate because we began to head toward Esther's for Sunday dinner. I glanced back and saw Peggy Norris follow Mr. MacDonald toward Inspector Grimsby. So far MacDonald and Grimsby hadn't noticed her listening to their conversation. I wondered what she would be complaining about when she got their attention.

Before we ate, James and Esther played with their children, egged on by Sir Henry, while running around the backyard. Adam held Stevie and my father sat next to him on a bench, telling Stevie what a good boy he was as if I'd given birth to a dog. Adam made room so I could squeeze onto the bench and sit next to both him and Stevie, holding them tight.

My father made a few stray comments to Adam and to Stevie. He didn't feel the need to say anything to me.

After an hour, we all went inside and washed our hands. It was a tight fit, but I enjoyed having everyone squeezed in around the dining room table in the Old Vicarage. We needed every plate in the house, mismatched as they were.

With all these people together, talking and laughing, the room was brighter than I remembered and warmer without being hot. It was as if the room, and by extension, the village, glowed.

There were so many of us that we ate the entire roast, not a difficult feat since it was wartime sized, that is, smaller than before the war. There were plenty of vegetables as well as warm apple slices in milk for afters.

All too soon, it was time for the three men to go back to London and the children to take their naps. James got the longest hugs from Esther and the children, and he was just going back to his office in London. It was a shadow of what I'd go through in another week. Time seemed to be galloping toward me.

Adam must have read my thoughts, since once he shook James's hand, he put his arm and one crutch around me and didn't let go. If my father was hoping for a long farewell with Adam, he wasn't going to get it, so he shook Adam's hand and rubbed Stevie's back, told me he'd see me next Sunday, and went to wait in the car.

It was only then I realized my father hadn't tried to hold Stevie even once. I guessed it was because Adam was so reluctant to let him go. Was my father escaping having to hold Stevie, which he didn't want to do, or was he being sensitive to Adam's craving to hold his son for the two weeks when he would have the chance?

"Adam, I'll give you a ride to London when the time comes," Sir Henry called out. "We'll work out the details next Sunday. All right if Sir Ronald and I come out next Sunday?"

"Much appreciated," Adam called back.

I appreciated it, too. Otherwise, Adam would have had to take the last bus on Thursday night to Oxford to catch the train to London to reach the meeting point in time on Friday morning.

Finally, at Sir Henry's urging, James climbed into the car and they drove off, all of us waving.

* * *

I will always remember those weeks as sunny and bright with warm breezes and smiling faces. When I said that to Esther later, she laughed and said didn't I remember the mist on Tuesday and the soaking rain on Wednesday, and Stevie's fussing all night Monday night until Magda cooked him an extra helping of mashed potatoes for breakfast on Tuesday.

None of that captured my attention. I just knew how I felt to have Adam around. To have him carry Stevie around the house and push his pram through the village. To hold me close at night. To talk about our future after the war, with a house in a village and more children.

In the evenings, we'd listen to the news on the wireless. I noticed Adam focused on the stories from Egypt and North Africa and Palestine. "That's where you're going," I whispered in his ear one evening.

He held me closer and grumbled a single sound. "Mmm." I knew he meant yes.

After that, I started scouring the newspapers for articles on Palestine and Egypt. I noticed Adam did too. "Are you studying Arabic?" I asked one evening.

"Have you seen me studying Arabic?"

"No, so I suspect you've been given two weeks off."

He smiled, which told me nothing and everything.

Every night as I shut my eyes, I tried to be thankful for our day together, but in the back of my mind, I felt the dread of being one day closer to Adam leaving me, perhaps forever.

His last night in Chipping Ford, as we lay intertwined in the dark silence, I finally found the nerve to ask, "They haven't declared you fit for battle, have they? You still use your crutches."

"No. I'll be doing what I've been doing all along, just on another continent. You're married to a cripple, for better or for worse."

"Is it safe? For you to go—wherever."

"We're in the middle of a war. Nowhere is safe."

"Doing what you do in a war zone."

"If the Blitz taught us anything, it's all a war zone." Then he pulled me tighter. "If it makes you feel better, I won't be anywhere near the front lines."

"Yes, it does. And promise me you'll be careful. Stevie and I need you."

"And I need you and Stevie, although he won't appreciate a father who can't run and play games the way James can."

I shifted around so I could look into his face, even if it was too dark to see his expression. "Just being there, to talk to, to read to him, to cheer him on, is more important than any game you might join in."

"It's a lifetime relationship, isn't it? I have to remember and focus on that." He ran a hand down my arm. "He's a cute child. Favors his mother."

"He has your eyes."

"I don't want to leave you, Livvy. You know that, don't you?"

"Yes. It doesn't mean I won't be upset, but I'm not

blaming you. Hitler, on the other hand, had better hope I don't catch up to him." I allowed myself to sound fierce and angry, letting loose all my hatred of the Fuhrer.

"The more of the army we can get out of England and trained and equipped elsewhere, the sooner we can start attacking—elsewhere. And now that the United States has entered the war, training and equipping at a rate that we can't, the sooner we can make some progress."

"Please, Adam, come home soon and in one piece."

"I want this war ended as soon as possible. I much preferred the peacetime army. I much prefer spending all my free time with you."

* * *

About dawn the next morning, Adam kissed Stevie where he slept in his cot and carried his sack downstairs while I made a pot of coffee. He drank a cup quickly, kissed me goodbye slowly, and then I stood on the front step and watched him walk out to Sir Henry's auto for a ride to London and then wherever the army planned to send him. I wasn't surprised to see my father sitting in the car.

Sir Henry and Adam waved to me, and I returned their waves. My father and I stared at each other.

When Magda rose, she found me sitting at the kitchen table with a cold half cup of coffee. She made a new pot and sat down next to me. "I am sorry, Livvy."

"I'm so afraid I'll never see him again." I swiped at my tears with my handkerchief.

"Some of us have been living with that since 1939. Earlier, even." She stood then and began work on breakfast, leaving me to wallow in my misery.

I knew she was German and Jewish and had to leave most of her family behind when she escaped to England. Usually, I could sympathize. I'd seen what had happened in Germany before the war. But I couldn't commiserate that morning.

Esther came in shortly afterward and sat next to me. "James hasn't gone overseas and probably won't. I can't imagine how that must feel. But if anyone can make a difference in this war, it's Adam. While you're feeling absolutely miserable, remember to feel very proud of him, too."

"I am proud of him. You can't guess how hard he worked to overcome his injuries from France to be able to stay in the army and play a role. At least I know he won't be on the front lines." And that was going to have to comfort me.

And I was going to pray the front lines didn't come to him.

Chapter Twenty-One

I spent the day feeding and changing Stevie, weeding the vegetable plot, and wondering exactly where Adam was. On a train? On a ship? On an airplane? Waiting for his transport?

Shortly before blackout, just as the sun set behind the hills, Mr. MacDonald knocked on our front door. I answered and let him in. It turned out Mrs. Coffey, his landlady, had run out of salt and she couldn't cook anything without salt. Magda folded a paper and poured salt into it and gave it to him.

As I showed him out into the darkness of the start of the night's blackout, Mr. MacDonald said, "This is a lifesaver. In a choice between over salted food and no food, I'll take over salted."

I burst out laughing. I felt terrible about Adam leaving, but it felt good to laugh. "She wouldn't really make you go hungry, would she?"

"Absolutely. She can't find her pots and pans until after she's found the salt."

I heard extra footsteps along the lane as Mr. MacDonald walked down the path to the gate with his shielded torch, but it was too dark to see who it was.

* * *

The first hint I had of anything being wrong was the next morning when I went to the shop to pick up our mail, and Lady Lydia snubbed me. Now, I really had no interest in talking to Lydia, but to be snubbed? That was strange. Usually, she addressed me as a medieval countess did to a peasant.

It was my turn at the counter next, and when I said to the postmistress that I had no idea why Lady Lydia was upset, she glared at me as she slammed our mail onto the counter and said, "Really?"

"Yes, really. I'd be glad to apologize to her if I knew what I was apologizing for."

"It's not her you need to apologize to."

"Did I offend Lady Agatha? Jane?"

"You can't be that foolish. Take your mail and go." She gathered our letters and threw them at me. "Next!"

I looked at her, mystified, as I gathered up the mail and walked to the door. At that moment, the baby's mother I had talked to at the last WI meeting I'd attended—whose name I never did get—opened the door and ran into me with her pram.

I stepped back, rubbing my shin, while she kept coming, rolling over my foot and walked past me without a word, as if I were invisible.

Fighting back tears of humiliation and pain, I raced out of the shop and across the green directly to Esther's house. I set the mail on the drawing room mantle and hurried out to where Esther and Goldie and the children were in the garden. When I reached the bench where Goldie was sitting, I burst into tears. "Everyone here hates me."

"Why?"

"I don't know. Lady Lydia snubbed me, then the postmistress was rude, and then some baby's mother ran me over with her pram and never spoke."

"Has this ever happened before?" Esther asked, coming over to us with Stevie in her arms.

"No. Everyone's been very nice to me before now. Well, before the meeting at the lodge."

"Maybe they think you owe Mrs. Brown-Dunn an apology," Esther said.

"Do I?" I asked her.

"That cow? I hope not," Goldie said.

Both Esther and I looked at the sweet, gentle woman in surprise.

"Since I don't speak around her, she doesn't realize how much English I understand. She says you should not trust me with your children, since I am a dirty German."

Before that moment, neither Esther nor I knew there

was a river of hate running through our village. Against the Germans, yes, in a vague, across-the-Channel type of way, but not against Jewish refugees. We both apologized to her for not knowing what had been said and for what was said.

"I wonder what else has been said, to make people react that way to me in the shop."

"We'll have to keep our ears open, Goldie, to see what else they say about us," Esther said.

It wasn't until late that afternoon when I was working in the garden that Mr. MacDonald came by and stood by the fence. "I thought I'd come along and say goodbye."

"A promotion to another office?" I knew I sounded surprised.

"No. I've been told someone complained about us. We've been indiscreet."

"What? No. Indiscreet? Whenever?" I rose and dusted off my knees before I walked over to the fence.

"The top brass at the manor had been told I've been making advances toward you, and you have responded."

"Good grief. Someone has been telling lies. But why?" Who needed Nazis when we had evil people in our village spreading gossip? I was furious. What if Adam heard this rubbish?

Mr. MacDonald leaned in and lowered his voice to a murmur. "I think it's because I'm getting close to proving a doctor… No. Never mind. I can't say anything. You understand. Official Secrets Act."

I began to suspect someone was hiding behind the Official Secrets Act. "Who is this doctor?"

"It wouldn't do for me to accuse this man without evidence."

"You're not. You haven't said anything about him. I just want to know his name in case it turns out to have a bearing on the murders."

"Dr. Embleton. He's a specialist in heart and lung diseases, but he has the highest rate of medical deferments in the country. If you repeat any of this, I'll deny it. It could be innocent. His patients are all sick, which is why they go to him and not a regular doctor."

"Of course." I thought I'd heard the name before, but I couldn't remember where. "But if they didn't want you to prove your case, they didn't need to drag my name into it. All of a sudden, this morning, I was snubbed and run over by a pram."

"A pram?" He sounded puzzled.

"Don't ask."

"I'm sorry you've been dragged into my little problem. It isn't fair that you are being talked about." MacDonald shook his head. "I've denied the story to the MOD, but they seem to believe there's no smoke without fire."

"It could be the other way around. I thought everyone was angry with me because I was trying to help the police find out who had killed a blackmailer."

"That would be her victims, surely."

"We couldn't find one of them. Which means that one…"

"Is the killer. And the inspector said to tell you it can't be Brenda from the pub. I had my eyes on her, along with several men from the manor house, when Mrs. Bryant was killed. Her cooking must be pretty awful, though, if she mistook autumn crocus for onions." Mr. MacDonald said, cringing.

"I've heard she was a good cook," I told him.

"Maybe she's not good at foraging."

I frowned. "Then the killer must be…"

Mr. MacDonald and I stared at each other for a full minute while I remembered where I'd heard the name Dr. Embleton. Then I said, "I know where I've heard of that doctor. And she has a son with a medical deferment. Could that be the secret worth killing to keep quiet?"

"But how would you prove it?" he replied.

"Does your unit work in conjunction with the local police?"

He nodded. "Of course."

"Tell them to contact Inspector Grimsby of Oxford about a murder he's investigating that might involve a medical deferment in Chipping Ford. And I'll pass a word to him from this end."

"I doubt I'll see you again, so stay safe, Mrs. Redmond."

"Good luck, Mr. MacDonald."

He walked off and I went back to my position on my

knees finishing the weeding. Within half a minute, Peggy Norris hurried past. Had she been watching us? Listening to us? I looked around, but I didn't see a spot where she could have been hidden but close enough to listen to us.

Still, I was suspicious. And I knew I couldn't keep my suspicions to myself.

After dinner, when I'd told Esther what I'd heard from Mr. MacDonald, I had her listen for Stevie while I ran up to the police constabulary.

Bell was in, his feet up on his desk, and he didn't bother to lower them when he saw it was me coming through the door. "Your soldier gone back to the front?"

"He has. Are you still in touch with Inspector Grimsby?"

"I am." His feet went down to the floor. "Do you have something for us?"

"At the manor, they have a unit looking at medical deferments. We have one young man who's been deferred in this village. And there's a doctor in common."

"Not Dr. Sampson."

"No. A doctor in Oxford. Specializes in heart and lung problems. Dr. Embleton."

"That would certainly get you a deferment."

"Yes. And most of his business is legitimate. It would have to be, or the MOD would have thrown him behind bars long ago. There's been a question about some patients, apparently, and Mr. MacDonald was looking into it. But now he's been reassigned because he was supposedly paying too much attention to me." I rolled my eyes.

Bell's eyes widened. "He was? What did your husband think?"

I gave him a look of disgust. "He wasn't. Adam didn't think anything. I don't know where the story started, but it has spread around the village and no one will speak to me now."

"Fallen woman, eh?" He gave me a grin.

"It's not funny, Constable. You can dislike me for a lot of things and you'd be right. But not anything that has to do with my marriage. Adam and I are very much in love."

"I didn't think you were the fallen woman type." Bell hurried to explain himself. "Nosy and bossy, maybe, with a touch of—"

"All right. Fine." I put my hand up. "I'm hard to get along with. But can you get this information to Grimsby?"

"He won't get it until Monday, probably." Bell wrote out all that I could tell him.

"Thank you. I'll be laying low, if you wonder where I am."

"Right you are. And be careful. There's still a killer in the village."

* * *

The next day was Sunday, and since Sir Henry wasn't coming out to the village this weekend, we planned to go to church. I wheeled Stevie up to the church and then inside and down the side aisle a row or two for a quick getaway if he started to fuss. Esther and her children slid in the pew from the other end on the main aisle.

A moment later, I heard someone in the row behind me, and I turned my head to see Jane sitting there with Andrew in his pram. "You certainly aren't popular," she murmured.

"So I've discovered. Do you know why?"

"You've apparently been cavorting with one of the men at the manor and deceiving your husband. You had to stop for the two weeks he was in town. And now your lover's being sent to another unit."

"Who?" I made clear I was scoffing at her news.

"MacDonald."

"Do you believe that?"

"Of course not. I found him to be friendly and talkative, too, but I wasn't helping the police."

"Lady Jane, come up here at once." We both turned to see Lady Lydia standing in the aisle beside her, hands on hips.

"It's a lie, Lady Lydia, and you might wonder why someone has started such a vile rumor," I said.

"You've been seen," she hissed.

"Doing what, exactly?" I said, glaring at her.

"Walking down the lane late at night with a man from the manor," she hissed at me.

"The police asked me to help them. They always made sure I was escorted if I had to be out with them after blackout. They didn't feel it was safe otherwise."

"This man isn't a policeman."

"The police think he is. Or are you telling the police who is a policeman and who isn't?" I was being snooty with Lydia and Esther shook her head slightly at me, while trying not to be obvious.

"Apparently, he wasn't, because the MOD people have sent him away."

"Somebody's been lying to the MOD people. And when they find out who it is, there's going to be trouble. I hope it's not you."

Before Lydia could reply, the organ began to play the first hymn, and she had to hurry down the side aisle to her row in front with Lady Agatha and Mrs. Brown-Dunn.

Behind me, I heard Jane give a quiet snort. "I need an hour away from them anyway," she said before she rose to sing the opening hymn.

The service was standard, average, without a hint of anything uplifting. We sang the hymns and listened to the readings and the sermon, but despite the rhetoric to bolster our resolve to fight the Nazi aggressors and defend our freedoms, we were left feeling flat. At least I was, and no one else appeared excited.

We waited to one side, Stevie sleeping as if he were an angel, Andrew starting to roll around in his pram, and Johnny trying to hit Becca with a prayer book, while the more nimble in the congregation went out into the sunshine. Lady Agatha, Mrs. Brown-Dunn, and Lydia came up to where we were still lingering and Lydia said, "Now you have everyone talking, Jane."

"Why would they be?" Jane asked, folding Andrew's blanket and setting it at the bottom of the pram.

"You sat in the back with—her."

"Lydia, you are hopeless. We're in the back because children can grow fussy in a moment. And Livvy hasn't done anything wrong. There are people in this village who have nothing better to do than gossip about their neighbors. When will the vicar preach on not bearing false witness against our neighbors? It's Livvy this week. Next week, it might be you," Jane warned her, then flapped a hand at her. "You'd better move. People want to go home for lunch."

Lydia aimed her nose at the heavens and marched out of the church. Lady Agatha was urged on by Mrs. Brown-Dunn taking a grip on her arm. She shook it off and said, "Mrs. Redmond, if you would call on me once your baby goes down for a nap this afternoon, I would appreciate it."

"Of course," I said and smiled, despite every muscle in my body shaking with trepidation. This would not be a pleasant meeting.

After that, the church quickly finished emptying and we could get the children out. Johnny saw a couple of small boys his age running to the green and he took off after them. Becca was stopped and forced by their mother to walk home with her rather than follow her older brother. Jane and I said goodbye until later and walked to our respective homes.

When Goldie and Magda heard about what was said in church, they were shocked. "Can you imagine if Lydia was the young earl's mother and not Jane?" Magda asked.

"She'd be impossible to live with in the same village," Goldie added as she headed out to collect Johnny for dinner.

"Lady Agatha has been the leader of local society for this entire century," I replied. "Why does she want to talk to me, and what can she do to me if she doesn't care for my answers?"

"I wondered why she ordered a new barrel of tar," Esther said and then started to laugh.

I wasn't laughing. I had nowhere else to go. My father didn't want me home, my flat had been bombed out at the end of the Blitz, and my husband was with the army somewhere overseas. I had to convince Lady Agatha to believe me.

Chapter Twenty-Two

Sunday dinner was pleasant, if not too flavorful or filling. Stevie had a little boiled mashed carrots and peas, along with his favorite mashed potatoes. The rest of us had some fish caught upstream and vegetables from the garden. Once we were finished and Stevie was down for his nap, I put on a little lipstick, set my hat at a jaunty angle, and went downstairs to be looked over by Esther.

"You look as if you are trying to send her a message that you are not going to be pushed around by an old hen," Esther told me.

"What do you think I should do?"

"Take off the lipstick, wear a cloche hat and gloves, and stand up straight."

"That last sounds good," I told her. We finally agreed I should remove my lipstick and set my wide-brim hat at a less provocative angle.

"Wear your gloves, too. You'd be surprised how much difference it makes."

I grabbed little white lace ones and walked up the street, wondering how many curtains twitched while people watched me climb the path to grovel at Lady Agatha's feet. But they were wrong. I wouldn't grovel, not even to the widow of an earl. If anything, Lydia should apologize to me.

Jane answered the door to my ring. Once again, I was slightly awed by the lodge's soaring entrance hall. When she saw me look around, she smiled and murmured, "Imagine trying to clean this."

Then she showed me into the main drawing room, where Lady Agatha sat in one of the chairs by the fireplace. She said, "Won't you join me, Mrs. Redmond?"

I took the other high-backed chair facing Lady Agatha's. They were close enough together to give a cozy feel in an otherwise vast space. We could keep our voices lowered and still hear each other clearly.

"There has been too much talk in the village these past few days," Lady Agatha began.

"Uninformed gossip," I replied.

"Is it?" Lady Agatha said and then, "Tea?"

"Please."

We sat in silence while she rang and asked for tea. After their maid left, she said, "Is there any truth to the rumors?"

"About my having an affair with Mr. MacDonald? Really? You can believe that?" I stared at Lady Agatha with raised eyebrows.

"It did seem rather farfetched, but I've been assured that it was Esther who called the manor house to complain about Mr. MacDonald's behavior."

"I assure you, it wasn't. There was nothing concerning Mr. MacDonald's behavior to complain about. He and my husband got on well. I think Mr. MacDonald is or was a policeman, before the war, because Inspector Grimsby called on his help a couple of times, including walking me home when I'd been out with the police at night with my camera."

"You understand why people might get the wrong impression."

"No, Lady Agatha, I don't. Someone made a call to the manor house pretending to be Esther with the expressed purpose of getting Mr. MacDonald into trouble. They don't want his investigation to continue."

We fell silent as the tea was brought in. Even after Lady Agatha poured the tea, we remained silent, watching each other from behind teacups. Finally, Lady Agatha said, "You suspect someone of evil intent."

"I do."

"But who? Why?"

"I don't know who, but I suspect it has something to do with Mr. MacDonald's work at the manor house."

"But no one knows what he was working on," Lady Agatha said, setting down her teacup on its saucer.

"Someone must know all the details. We know it involves someone or something that has come to the attention of the police in Oxford, because Inspector Grimsby is based there and he was involved in Mr. MacDonald's work. We know the phone call must have been made locally, because it wasn't a trunk call according to the constable, so it involves someone in the village. Now, how many people in the village have frequent dealings in Oxford? Or how many people know who is working on what at the manor?" I hoped Lady Agatha had the answer, because I didn't know how many people I had described.

"And how many people want to run you out of this village, or at least silence you?" She studied me for a moment. "Who have you made an enemy of? When we can answer that, we'll be able to find the person who made that telephone call."

"Half the village thinks I've made an enemy of you," I told her.

"Nonsense. We'll simply have to correct that notion. Come to the WI meeting this week and I'll put a stop to that."

"Thank you." It would make my life easier.

Lady Agatha wasn't going to let the question of who had started this campaign against me go. "I feel an obligation to the people of Chipping Ford, particularly with a murderer on the loose. Do you have any idea who has a connection to Oxford?"

"A connection that also has a connection to what Mr.

MacDonald is investigating. I've heard a rumor that Mr. MacDonald's work is involved with a particular doctor selling medical deferments for military service. And I've made enemies of people in this village while I've tried to stop a murderer who silenced a blackmailer. No, I don't know who it is, but I wonder if Inspector Grimsby does."

"Selling medical deferments for military service? No, that cannot be allowed. I lost both my sons in this war. Whatever help you need to stop this, I will be glad to provide." It was the first time I'd seen Lady Agatha appear angry.

After we finished our tea, I thanked Lady Agatha and headed to the constabulary house. Fortunately, Constable Bell was in.

"You've created quite a stir in the village," he greeted me.

"And all it took was a phone call claiming to be from Esther." I glared at him.

"The call was made from the public telephone box just outside the village beyond the manor house. No way we could prove that she did or didn't make that call."

"Strange that she'd make the call from the box when we have a telephone in our front hall."

"That would have been too obvious," Bell said. "We'd have traced it straight back to your house."

"Inspector Grimsby was involved in Mr. MacDonald's work, wasn't he?"

"Yes." Constable Bell leaned back in his chair.

"We know it had something to do with someone in the town."

"A doctor. You told me that."

I leaned over Bell's desk. "Dr. Embleton is a heart and lung doctor. He has given a large number of medical deferments from the military. Enough for the military to become suspicious."

"Wouldn't all his patients be deferred? You don't go to a heart and lung doctor if there isn't a problem."

"In most cases that's true, Constable, but if you wanted to buy a deferment, who better to grant it?"

Bell sat up and began looking through his notebook. "In old Dr. Forrester's notes, we have one young man with some asthma who then went to Dr. Embleton."

"Does this young man have a medical deferment now and when did he receive it? And was his mother part of the blackmail and murder investigation that you and Inspector Grimsby carried out?" I found I had to lead Bell along to notice the connections that were obvious. Well, obvious to me.

Bell looked up from his notebook. "I'll find out in the morning when offices reopen and I can attempt to reach the inspector again."

"Then I'll talk to you tomorrow, Constable, after you talk to the inspector." I gave him a smile. "I think we're getting to the bottom of our murder. Something we'd never be able to do if the murderer wasn't busy blowing smoke in our faces."

"Sooner or later, criminals always make a mistake. Thank goodness. You be careful until we know for certain who we're after."

"Oh, I will. I have no desire to be the killer's next victim," I told him. I left the constabulary, looking forward to dressing in something more casual.

The rest of the day, we baked some teething biscuits for Stevie along with some fruit-sweetened biscuits for Johnny and Becca. Once they cooled, we all watched as Stevie gnawed on one of his, slobbering and making faces that made us all laugh.

We had beans and toast with vegetables from the garden for supper and then listened to the radio after our meal. Stevie showed a fondness for teething biscuits and had to have one before bed, which meant the other two children had to eat one of their biscuits before they would lie down.

"This isn't going to happen every night," Esther warned her two. With Stevie teething, I couldn't make such a vow.

After they all finally settled down, Esther and I went back downstairs to listen to the news on the radio. "Things are certainly heating up in north Africa and Palestine," I commented after one positive report.

"It's good to know Adam is taking a role in getting our forces ready," Esther said.

"I'd rather he was in England," I responded sourly.

"But I imagine he's happier in the field. He is regular army. James will never be more than a pencil pusher in a uniform."

I laughed. "I doubt James would care to hear you say that."

"He admits it, at least to me. I know he's thankful we have men in this country with Adam's talents. Who know what they're doing."

I was proud to hear her say that, even as I worried about him.

When we went to bed, I opened the window a little since the night still seemed to be warm. When I awoke, it was still dark out, but the air was irritating my nose and mouth. Pollen, I thought. Something I was not used to. London smelled more of coal fires and mold.

I rose and shut the window. There was a light on in the doctor's surgery down the lane. Nothing unusual in that. Sampson wrote out his notes at the end of the day or immediately after a difficult case. His legs pained him in the same way Adam's did, so I understood how he couldn't get much sleep even if he wanted to.

I crawled back into bed, twisting and turning since it was hot in our front bedroom with the window shut. Eventually, unable to sleep, I rose again and went to the window.

There was something wrong with the light in the doctor's surgery. Had he knocked over a lamp? The light seemed to flicker now. I opened the window and immediately sneezed. That wasn't pollen, that was smoke.

I threw a sweater and skirt over my nightgown and ran into Esther's room. "Wake up," I whispered. "Fire."

"Wha-? Huh?" Then she sat bolt upright. "Fire?"

"Fire at the doctor's surgery. Can you get Constable Bell and the fire brigade? I'll go try to rouse Dr. Sampson."

I hurried downstairs to Esther's louder "What?" behind me. I pulled on my wellies by the side door and slipped outside.

The sky was dark and full of stars, and while I couldn't see smoke, I could smell it. I hurried down the lane and across to the doctor's house and banged on the door. No lights or sound from inside. I banged again and then raced to the door to the surgery.

The knob opened easily in my hand. I walked in to find the filing cabinets in the far corner that held Dr. Forrester's records on fire.

I turned on the sink in the examination room and filled a shallow metal pan normally used for instruments. Then running into the other room, spilling half the water, I threw it on the open file cabinet drawers.

Spinning around, I raced back, filled the pan again and dumped it on the fire.

With the addition of water, the smoke in the room was getting thicker and the flames were shorter.

I didn't see who came into surgery, but I heard them as

I filled the pan again. "Find a pail and fill it with water for dowsing the flames," I shouted, hurrying across the wet floor to deliver another soaking to the burning records.

Turning again, I ran into Peggy Norris. "Quick, find a pail," I shouted, shoving her out of the way on my way to the sink. Filling the pan, I hurried back into the office.

I was halfway across when I was shoved and fell onto the wet floor, throwing the water uselessly onto the bottom drawers of the filing cabinets. I rolled over to find Mrs. Norris lighting the papers on the desk.

I'll never forget the smile on her face when she pushed the flaming papers onto me.

I pushed them off me and onto the wet floor. My hands screamed in pain where the papers burned them. I leaped up with a scream before Mrs. Norris shoved more burning paper onto me.

I threw the embers back into her face and hair.

She cried out and blundered into the examination room to put her head under the sink tap.

Spluttering, she stood up and came after me, a scalpel in her hand. I used the pan to fight her off, a dull clang each time pan met scalpel. Peggy Norris forced me back toward the still-smoldering filing cabinets, the smoke thicker with each step I made in retreat.

My lungs burned and my throat ached. *Don't start coughing. Don't cough. Don't.*

Chapter Twenty-Three

I couldn't stop myself. I started coughing. My only defense was to keep swinging the pan in the direction of the blade.

Then Peggy Norris rushed toward me with the scalpel extended. I leaped to the side, a sharp pain running down my arm as she ran past and screamed as she slipped on the wet floor and collided with the smoldering file cabinets. Embers rained down on her.

I turned to run and escape her attack, only to collide with Esther. Constable Bell grabbed Peggy Norris and pulled her away from the fiery cabinets. He led her to the sink and splashed water over her.

Meanwhile, Esther was frantically searching the examination room for bandages to cover the slice in my arm from the scalpel and stop the bleeding. "Where's Dr. Sampson?" I asked her.

Bell answered for her. "He was called out to a farm

toward Chipping Upham as I was making my evening rounds. An elderly farmer with breathing difficulties."

"This is the best I can do until he returns. I think you may need stitches, Livvy," Esther said.

Peggy Norris patted herself dry and shouted, pointing at me, "She did this. She set the fire and tried to burn me."

"I told Esther I saw the flames over here before I came over and sent her to get the constable. And then you dumped burning paper on me and went after me with a scalpel." I sounded angry, fueled by the pain in my arm.

"Liar." Her lips curled in disgust. Did she really believe her version of events?

"The fire was burning well before Livvy left the house. I know. I smelled the smoke and looked out," Esther said.

"Everyone knows you two stick up for each other." Peggy Norris turned on her heel and marched out of the surgery, Constable Bell hurrying after her.

"You need to make a formal statement," I heard him call out.

I couldn't hear her reply over Esther filling a deeper pan, which she carried over to the filing cabinets to extinguish any remaining embers. "Thick paper such as this doesn't burn as readily. If it had enough time, it would have charred all of it, but a lot of this has survived," she told me.

"Let's spread it out to dry so all these wet sheets don't mat together," I suggested, and we set to work.

The fire brigade came clanging up the hill and rushed in

with hose and ax. We showed them the fire was out and we were now trying to save what records we could. After assuring themselves that no hot embers remained, they left, warning us to be careful.

Constable Bell rejoined us as they left. After the men talked for a minute, Bell came in and began to help separate records, complaining about Mrs. Norris and her "unhelpful attitude."

I could hardly believe he let her walk free. Could he possibly believe her about what had happened? She had assaulted me. Did he believe her over me? I was furious.

A great deal of the old records was damaged by either fire or water or both, but even more appeared to be undamaged. We couldn't tell how much had been completely destroyed. We had most of it spread out over desks, chairs, cabinets, and the floor of the examination room when Dr. Sampson came in, looking perplexed.

"There's a nationwide petrol shortage and I get called miles out of my way as a prank," he said grumbling. Then he looked around. "Has there been a fire? What happened?"

I started telling him what I'd smelled and seen, ending with the cut on my arm and the arrival of Esther and the constable.

"You say Peggy Norris set the fire to the old records? But why? If she was in here, she could have just taken her records home with her. I seldom look at them. I never would have noticed."

"But we looked at them," I reminded him. "If we wanted to look at them again, we'd have noticed if hers were specifically missing."

"Then this fire wouldn't have happened if you hadn't looked through those records against my wishes," Dr. Sampson said. Despite the anger in his tone, his touch was gentle as he unwrapped and examined my cut arm.

"After she murdered Mrs. Bryant, she might have done anything," I replied.

"Mrs. Norris murdered Mrs. Bryant?" Esther said, her voice rising.

I nodded. "I've asked the constable to have Inspector Grimsby and Mr. MacDonald come out here in the morning. Then I'll explain everything to them, since the murder is all wrapped up with their work in Oxford."

"And Mrs. Withins?" Esther asked, quietly this time.

"I think she saw Mrs. Norris at Mrs. Bryant's and either told her so, or tried to blackmail her with that knowledge."

After he finished rewrapping my wound, Dr. Sampson surveyed the damage to his surgery and then said, "We might as well head to our beds if you're finished sorting out the records."

"Who phoned you about this prank emergency?" I asked him.

"A woman. I think. The voice was muffled."

"The same as the call accusing you and Mr. MacDonald of shameful behavior," the constable said. "Should be interesting to see if the same call box was used for both."

"But that's not the closest one to the Norris cottage," Dr. Sampson protested. "Shouldn't that mean it wasn't her?"

"The closest one is on the green, in full view of the pub and the post office. The one past the manor house isn't visible to anyone except a few people at shift change in the MOD offices. You could make a call from that box and practically guarantee not to be seen," the constable said.

"That's all good and well, but I'm for my bed. Close up after yourselves." Dr. Sampson slowly walked to the door that connected the surgery with his living quarters and let himself in, shutting the door firmly behind him.

"Good advice. The fire is definitely out and the papers that are left are drying. Let's get some sleep," Esther said as she headed outside.

"Keep an eye on her, Mrs. Powell. I think Mrs. Redmond has a target on her back, especially since we hope the inspector and Mr. MacDonald will be returning in the morning." The constable ushered me out and shut and locked the door behind us.

"Where did you find the key? The door was unlocked when I arrived," I asked him.

"Mrs. Norris had it. She dropped it when I was rinsing the embers out of her hair," Bell said.

"How did she end up with...?" Esther asked.

"When she went after me with the scalpel, I moved out

of the way and she slipped on the water on the floor and collided with the file cabinets." Fortunately. If she hadn't, she could have done much worse than slice my arm before Bell and Esther showed up.

Bell walked us to the garden gate and then headed home while we went inside. "I don't know if I'll sleep tonight as I listen for Peggy Norris to break in," Esther said.

"Magda will be up soon and she'll hear if anyone breaks in," I said. "I shall try to sleep well." I went up to my room and took off my sweater and skirt only to find I had to change my now wet and bloody nightgown. Then I lay down and found my arm hurt too much to sleep.

The sky was growing light by the time I did drop off. When I woke up, alive and grateful for it, it was late and the village was busy with daily life.

I cleaned up, fed Stevie, and after I dressed him and changed his nappy, we went downstairs. Magda had mushed up a little cooked apple for Stevie, plus he and I shared some oat porridge.

Everyone in the household was already awake and had heard about the fire at the doctor's surgery and Mrs. Norris attacking me with a scalpel.

Johnny greeted me with "I want to be a fireman."

"You'd enjoy the excitement, but I don't think you'd care for the flames," I told him. "They hurt."

Becca was more fascinated with my bandaged arm. "You have an owie."

"I do, indeed."

"Did you have to have stitches?" Goldie asked.

"Fortunately, no. It wasn't wide nor deep, so Dr. Sampson thinks keeping it wrapped tightly will let it mesh back together."

"You'll end up with a scar," Magda declared ominously.

"My own war wound," I replied in a grimace.

"We're going to have to keep an eye on Livvy until the police take Mrs. Norris into custody. And that won't happen until the inspector and Mr. MacDonald arrive," Esther told them.

"I could use some help in the kitchen this morning, and Stevie is always welcome, aren't you, little one," Magda said, patting Stevie on the head.

As it turned out, by the time we finished breakfast and washing dishes, I didn't even have enough time to chop all the vegetables for Woolton pie before the knock on the door. I left Stevie in the kitchen and went to open the door until Esther stopped me and looked out the window.

"It's the inspector," she said and walked away, letting me open the door to the two men outside.

"How are you, Mrs. Redmond?" Mr. MacDonald asked as he entered, his hat in his hand.

"A little shaken and my arm hurts. No lasting damage," I told him. "Won't you come in, Mr. MacDonald? Inspector Grimsby?"

"Let's get a statement from you about what happened

last night at the doctor's surgery," Grimsby said.

"Of course." I led them into the drawing room and after we sat and Grimsby took out his notebook, I began telling them, in the best order I could, the events of the previous night.

Grimsby questioned everything and wrote down every detail. Then he said, "Right now, Bell should be questioning Mrs. Norris."

"Why do you think Mrs. Norris would attack you?" Mr. MacDonald said.

"She was trying to burn all the old doctor's records and I tried to stop her. She didn't want me to."

"And why would she try to destroy Dr. Forrester's records? No one looks at those."

"Constable Bell and I have. There are old medical records about her son and they don't mention any heart ailment. Just some asthma."

"You know what my task is for the MOD." MacDonald made it a statement.

"Yes."

"Asthma would be enough to keep him out of the regular forces. That should be enough to satisfy anyone," Mr. MacDonald said.

"But not out of the auxiliary forces. He could push papers in uniform here or abroad. Well back from the front lines, if there is such a thing in this war," I said.

MacDonald nodded. "There are a great number of tasks

he could take over if he were fit for them."

"Do we know when Benjamin Norris received his deferment?" I asked.

MacDonald rattled off a date. "Before Dr. Sampson fired Mrs. Bryant."

"Shortly before the newest stream of blackmail payments began to arrive in Mrs. Bryant's bank account and appear in her record book," Grimsby added. "More circumstantial evidence, but it points us in the right direction."

"Mrs. Norris refuses to entertain the thought of her son in uniform. Or traveling far from home. She doesn't want to let him go. It's sad, when you think about it," I said.

"Is he an only child?"

"No, she has a daughter who's younger, but her son is the one she worries about."

"I'll deny it if you tell anyone," MacDonald said, "but we have enough to require young Mr. Norris to take another physical from one of our doctors. Also several other of Dr. Embleton's patients."

"Will he go to jail?"

"That depends on whether he cooperates with us." Mr. MacDonald smiled slightly. "And how good his solicitor is."

"And Mrs. Norris?"

"If we can prove a case against her for killing Mrs. Bryant or Mrs. Withins, she'll hang," Grimsby said.

I shuddered. One more death in this time of war.

Although it would mean I would be safe from Peggy Norris's attacks. And Mrs. Withins certainly didn't deserve killing. She wasn't a blackmailer, was she? At least not that anyone could prove.

"Does this mean you'll be coming back to the village and working at the manor house again?" I asked Mr. MacDonald.

"No, I imagine both Grimsby and I will be working from Oxford from now on. Or at least once it is decided whether charges can be brought against Mrs. Norris."

I heard a knock on the door and excused myself to answer it. I was surprised to see Constable Bell standing on the step, looking hot and out of breath. "What is it?"

"Is the inspector here?" he asked pushing past me.

I followed him into the drawing room in time to hear him say, "Mrs. Norris has vanished."

Chapter Twenty-Four

Inspector Grimsby leaped to his feet. "Disappeared, has she? Why didn't you lock her up last night? Put out a wire to all police that she needs to be apprehended."

"There was no reason to think she'd take off. She's lived here all her life," Bell said.

"Do we know where her son is?" Mr. MacDonald asked.

"No. Only the daughter was home. And she wouldn't tell me anything," Bell said.

"Mother must have coached her well." Grimsby headed past me into the hall. "Thank you, Mrs. Redmond. We'll take it from here. I don't think she'll bother you anymore."

The men left, Mr. MacDonald squeezing my hand in sympathy. As soon as I shut the door, Esther and Magda appeared. "I think we ought to keep our guard up for a while. There's no telling where Mrs. Norris is now," Esther said.

I nodded. "At least for a few days. They're sure to find her soon."

"And what can she do?" Esther asked. "There are four of us and only one of her."

"What about her son?"

"She hasn't allowed him to get mixed up in any of her assaults so far. She won't start now," Esther said with more certainty than I felt.

* * *

The next several days went on as they would in any English village during the war. Lady Agatha, showing she had faith in me, suggested me for the chairperson of the WI autumn bazaar jam stall, which was immediately agreed by the rest of the assembly.

"I don't know anything about making jam," I whispered to Jane over our prams.

"Just praise everyone who offers to help and ask their advice. Never express your own opinions, only ask for theirs. There's quite a rivalry involved in jam making here. Don't show any favoritism and you'll do fine," she told me.

"Does Lady Agatha hate me?" I asked.

"No. She's showing great trust in you and your ability to handle divergent opinions in the village."

"What does that mean?" I must have looked confused. I certainly felt that way.

"She thinks you're clever and you handle yourself well."

"Wow, thanks, Jane." I was getting the feeling that if it weren't for the honor, I would regret my new position. I suspected managing the jam stall would call for tact and diplomacy equal to ending a war. I hoped I wouldn't meet the same fate as Chamberlain.

"And she's showing the village she trusts you." Jane gave me a broad smile.

After the meeting, I was given the schedule leading up to the WI autumn bazaar and its jam stall while Esther waited for me. We posted the bazaar schedule in the kitchen.

Beyond that, our lives revolved around the garden, the kitchen, the laundry, and the post office. When I was feeling restless, I would push Stevie in his pram and watch the children play on the village green. The mothers of the younger children, including Esther, would sit on the benches and keep watch while exchanging recipes and gossip.

Sometimes I would join them, my supposed fall from grace forgotten. Occasionally, I was asked if there'd been any word about Mrs. Norris, followed by how sad her daughter appeared. Gossip said her aunt had offered her a home and then later her uncle had, but she had sent them both away.

Lady Lydia thought it was shameful, the girl living on her own, and wanted to get the authorities involved. Since Lydia couldn't get anyone else to do it, and she would never stoop to interfering on her own, nothing was done, although some of the women took the girl dinner on a rotating basis.

The school said she was very quiet, but she was keeping up with her schoolwork, this being the end of the school year, and that made its way around the village in the gossip circle, too.

All of this made me suspicious about where Mrs. Norris and her son were, but since no one had spotted them, I began to believe they were far away from Chipping Ford. Still, we kept the doors locked.

Two weeks later, during a time when I'd only received one heavily redacted letter from Adam in his new post where the postmark was in Arabic, I received a visit from Inspector Grimsby. He sat in our drawing room and stared at me for a minute. "We don't know where Mrs. Norris or her son are."

"You should, shouldn't you? We're at war, our ports and air fields are watched. Everyone is on the watch for strangers." Grimsby couldn't have brought worse news.

"Yes, we should. She must have a friend or relative far from here, perhaps in Scotland or Ireland, who is hiding them."

"Do you think you'll find her?"

"Eventually. She'll get in touch with her daughter sometime. She can't just leave a thirteen-year-old alone indefinitely, and yet she seems to have ordered the girl to stay home. When she contacts her, we'll have her."

"You're certain she will."

"Yes. And if she doesn't soon, we'll take the girl into care. Leave the house empty and lock it up from the outside."

"And then watch it?"

"Oh, yes. Just in case. Meanwhile, we're keeping an eye on Scotland and Ireland. Ireland would probably be her best bet for hiding her son, but we've not been able to find any connection between any of them and any person or place in Ireland." He studied me for a minute. "Do you think you could ask around? Find the link for us?"

"I'll try. You're sure she's the murderer?"

"We can now show Mrs. Bryant was blackmailing Mrs. Norris about her son's medical deferment. We have evidence from the bank that Mrs. Norris paid Dr. Embleton a huge sum for routine medical care, indicating payment for a fake deferment, and that he received similar payments for treatment of other young men. She set fire to Dr. Forrester's records, although she didn't manage to burn her son's records. Records that show he wasn't born with or later display a heart condition."

"She made a mistake there, not wiping out all of the records."

"She would have if you hadn't been awakened by the smoke and gone to investigate."

I was glad I had. She had killed two people to hide her secret and unsettled an entire village.

And yet she'd escaped and left her young daughter behind. It didn't make sense.

"Will you be staying in the village for a while?" I asked.

"No. We're getting the prosecution ready for both Mrs.

Norris and Dr. Embleton from the headquarters in Oxford."

I saw Inspector Grimsby off shortly before lunch. When we all sat around the table, passing the shepherd's pie, I asked Esther, very quietly, who would know of anyone Mrs. Norris knew in Ireland.

"Her brother had a farmhand from Ireland once. It wasn't long before the war. You might ask Tom or Rose Johnson. Oh, wait. I believe Rose is originally from Ireland."

"Mrs. Norris's sister-in-law is Irish? I don't know either Tom or Rose except possibly by sight."

"You can't go emptyhanded, and since they live on a farm outside the village, vegetables wouldn't do any good. Magda, could we do with buying a few eggs off one of the farms nearby?" Esther asked.

"We can always do with a few more eggs," Magda said drily.

"There you go. Take a couple of sixpences with you and buy us some extra eggs." Then Esther dug into her shepherd's pie with relish.

After lunch, they outfitted me with a basket lined and covered with hand towels and sent me on my way. I was only stopped twice by members of the WI, who asked where I was going and why.

It was a warm afternoon, and following Esther's directions, I must have looked damp and red-faced by the time I arrived at the Johnson farm. Rose, wiry and red-faced herself, was scrubbing out her oven, the door to the outside propped open. "Mrs. Redmond, what brings you out here?"

"Hello, Mrs. Johnson. I heard you might have a few eggs I could buy."

"Well, I don't have very many. How many do you need?"

"Just a few."

"Hens don't care to lay in this heat."

"So we've noticed." And then I noticed it. And gave a silent cheer. "Are you from Ireland, Mrs. Johnson? I think I detect a bit of an Irish accent."

"And here I thought I'd lost all of my accent."

"You still have a little left. What part are you from?"

"South of Belfast." Her voice lost its welcome.

"County Down?" I asked.

"Do you know it?"

"I was on the Ards peninsula for a story for the *Daily Premier*. Are you from there?" I asked with a smile.

"No. More inland."

"It's beautiful country. At least the peninsula was."

"It's beautiful country," she agreed. That seemed to determine it. "Let's go find you, say, three eggs?"

"That would be most helpful, Mrs. Johnson."

Once I received the eggs and paid, I asked, "Is your niece coming to stay with you once the school year ends?"

"She's finally agreed. I think she's tired of living in the cottage on her own."

My elation sped my feet back to the village in the heat. Once I'd given Magda the eggs, I went up the hill to the constabulary house.

For once, Inspector Grimsby had let Constable Bell sit in his own chair behind his desk. He was in the guest chair, staring at me. "You were successful."

"Rose Johnson, sister-in-law to Peggy Norris, is from County Down in Northern Ireland. I think you'll find the Norrises are there."

"How did you work that out?" Bell asked.

"Have you never noticed her accent?" I asked.

"Oh. Yes. I'd forgotten that."

Grimsby and I both looked at him in disbelief.

"Well, what's her maiden name?" Grimsby asked.

"I don't know, and I didn't see any way to ask," I told him.

"It's…O'Neill," Constable Bell said after a pause.

"How did you know that?" I asked.

"This is a village. A new person coming to live here, marrying a local, particularly ten years ago, was a nine days' wonder. I might not have been a constable here for a long time but I've been a resident all my life."

"And Peggy Norris has lived here all her life. You believed her story rather than mine the night of the fire, didn't you, Constable?"

"You're a newcomer. Living with other newcomers and foreigners. We tend to trust our own." He looked away from me.

"And so a murderer is running free." I glared at him. I

didn't appreciate not being believed, and now I knew not to trust Bell in anything to do with the murders.

"I'll call Oxford and get them to contact the police in Belfast. I hope this wraps up the case," Grimsby said. "Any fishing boat could cross the Irish Sea and never be noticed by our officials."

"I hope it wraps up our murders," I told them. "I don't enjoy living with a need to constantly look over my shoulder."

"You shouldn't have to much longer. Bell will let you know when we pick them both up."

I went home feeling relieved, if not certain Bell would ever tell me.

In the days that followed, life in Chipping Ford took on a slower, calmer pace. Warm breezes made everyone think of holidays before the war spent at beach resorts. Letters came infrequently from the far end of the Mediterranean, but I did hear from Adam on occasion. Vegetables, fruits, and flowers led to more honey production, and Stevie developed a taste for sweetened porridge, sweetened mushed vegetables, and playing with Esther's children. He was growing quickly, and I took another picture of him every week or so.

I was also taking photographs of other children to send to their fathers away in the service of King and Country. This way I finished a roll of film every month or so and the other mothers would chip in for the developing and the next roll of film. The post office on the green was never as busy as the day after I'd get developed film returned to me.

Slowly, the Yanks were filling up an air base in the next county with American airplanes and American jeeps and American music and chewing gum. It didn't affect us in Chipping Ford directly, but there was always some news or gossip that made us feel as if we were no longer standing alone. As if there would be an end to this never-ending war.

The youngsters in the village quickly developed a taste for American music and American dancing while snapping their chewing gum.

But with all these foreigners at the air base, we continued to lock our doors, at least after dark.

The sun shone and the temperatures went up and the children played outdoors and we were all a little more cheerful. Until my father came to visit along with Sir Henry.

We went out in the early Sunday sunshine to greet them as they pulled up outside of our gate. Esther looked for James, and not seeing him, pouted a little. My father, seeing her reaction, said, "With the Yanks arriving, James is busier than ever. He hardly gets time to sleep. You should be proud of the work he's doing."

"I am," came out through clenched lips.

By now my father knew he'd made an etiquette error with his hostess. To cover his embarrassment, he went to pick up Stevie. Stevie had been fussing all night as he cut teeth and had refused to go to Nanny Goldie or Esther so I could eat my breakfast.

The moment Stevie felt his grandfather's hands taking him by the middle, he let out a howl of epic volume. My father jumped back, letting him go. It was all I could do to keep from dropping my precious baby.

"Watch what you're doing," I snapped. "You could hurt him if you drop him." I glared at my father and marched inside.

"I didn't mean…" he said to Esther, who walked past, ignoring him.

I heard his muffled voice mixing with Sir Henry's from outside, and then they both came in. "Shall we sit, have a cup of tea, and try to have a pleasant conversation?" Sir Henry said.

"I'm very sorry about Stevie," my father said. "That was my fault. Do you want me to leave?"

"Yes, but that's not fair to Esther or Sir Henry. Just sit there and let me get over my fright. And Stevie's," I told him.

After that, we had a reasonably pleasant visit. We moved out into the back garden while Johnny and Becca played with their grandfather. My father attempted to entertain Stevie while he sat on my lap until Magda called us all in for dinner.

We went in and reverted to our ordinary habits. No one locked the kitchen door.

Chapter Twenty-Five

Sunday dinner was tasty, thanks to Magda's skill in the kitchen. My father realized Stevie wasn't going to let go of me and began to relax, impressed by the child's appetite. "He's changed a great deal since I saw him last," he admitted.

"Teething, growth spurt, bad mood. I don't know what I'm getting from one day to the next. I'm having to learn to accept all these changes," I told him.

"We don't know what we're signing up for when we become parents," my father said.

"That is so true," Sir Henry said as Johnny and Becca started to bicker and Esther tried to intervene.

After the meal, I cleaned Stevie up and set him in his pram. My father and I walked him around the green while Sir Henry and his grandchildren ran around the center. "Do they ever play cricket on the pitch anymore?" my father asked.

"The schoolboys do, assisted on occasion by men working at the manor house. Once or twice, the men have played. As with so many other things, cricket will have to wait for the end of the war."

"Have they caught that woman murderer in the village?" my father asked, dropping his voice.

"Not that I've heard, but they think they know where she and her son are. Do you know she left her thirteen-year-old daughter behind when she ran?"

"Good grief. The poor child. Is she away at school?"

I shook my head. "She's staying with her uncle's family now that the school year has ended and the authorities threatened to take her into care." And then I thought, her mother is with the girl's aunt's family. That would make it easier for mother and daughter to communicate undetected through relatives.

My father frowned. "What's wrong?"

"Nothing. I just noticed a connection I hadn't considered. No matter, it's not our worry." I turned the pram and started back the other way.

Sir Henry planned to start out so he could get the car parked at his London home before blackout, and my father had tired of the countryside, and my company, long before then. The weather was so warm and dry, however, that Stevie ended up taking his nap in his pram and Becca, who still needed an afternoon nap, didn't get one because Sir Henry and Johnny were having such a good time that neither wanted to say goodbye.

Finally, however, my father gave me a generous amount of money to "help out," showing he still felt guilty about almost dropping his grandson, and then he and Sir Henry drove off with a jaunty wave. Magda called us in for supper, bread and cheese for the rest of us and some mashed veggies with cheese for Stevie, and then Becca fell asleep almost before she rose from the table.

All the fresh air had made Stevie tired as well, and he went down in his cot easily. Once he was asleep, making cute little noises, I went downstairs. Esther was still upstairs with Johnny, who was too excited from playing with his grandfather to go to sleep.

The radio was on some orchestral program and Nanny Goldie was asleep with her feet up on a footstool. I went into the kitchen to see if Magda wanted to listen to the radio, planning to offer to do the dishes for her, but she wasn't there. Then I realized she hadn't finished the dishes.

That was something Magda would never do.

I walked back to her room and knocked on the door. "Magda, are you all right?"

Hearing no answer, I opened her door a few inches. Magda sat across the room from me, on the other side of her bed, with a gag tied around her mouth.

I pushed the door open further and took one step forward when I realized Magda was watching a spot to the left of me. Behind her door.

I slammed the door open as hard as I could and let out a scream that should have wakened our neighbors in the graveyard. A responding groan of pain came from behind the door.

Stepping away from the door, I closed it partway and found Peggy Norris on the floor, bleeding freely from where a knife was stuck in her side.

Fortunately, it looked to be a small blade.

Goldie came in behind me and I heard Esther's footsteps running down the stairs. At a nod, Goldie went to free Magda's mouth, followed by her bound hands and feet.

"Get Dr. Sampson and then Constable Bell," I told Esther as she entered the room and looked around her in shock. She looked at Peggy Norris, whose blouse was now stained red and wet with blood and turned away, gagging, on her way to the doctor's house.

I knelt next to the stricken woman and said, "Mrs. Norris, we've gone to get the doctor. You need to hold very still so the knife doesn't shift."

"Ben is safe," she gasped out, managing to sound haughty. "They can't touch him."

"I know. Your sister-in-law, Rose Johnson, told me he was in Ireland." Mrs. Johnson hadn't, but I had guessed at his location and wondered if she'd admit it.

"She had no business..." she began and then a sharp gasp stopped her words. She had shifted and now made a sound between a groan and a snore.

"Just be quiet. Don't move. The doctor should be here any second." I hoped. She was pale and sweating and I had no idea what to do. Blood was seeping out of her side faster now.

"This was meant for you," came out very quietly. I think I was the only person to hear it, but I know I was the only person she wanted to hear her words. The anger in her eyes told me how much she had wanted to plunge the knife into me.

"Did you kill Mrs. Bryant and Mrs. Withins to keep Ben safe?" I asked.

"If I didn't keep paying, Phyllis Bryant would have told. She had to die. As you should have. Ben can come back after the war. He'll be safe and whole. No one should interfere with that."

"And Mrs. Withins?"

Another gasp as she flinched from the pain. I didn't think she'd answer me until she said, "She found Phyllis Bryant's record book. When she saw me go into her house, she knew why. She wanted to continue on the same terms." She shook her head and something vaguely similar to a laugh came out. "If I killed Phyllis to stop her taking my money, why would I agree to pay someone else?"

Dr. Sampson came in and in one glance, took in the entire scene. Then his only focus was on Peggy Norris. I got out of the way for him and then at his command, left to get him a basin of hot water and towels.

Magda followed me out, the door being half open, and went to the kitchen to give me the towels I could use to sop up blood and to start heating water. I heard Constable Bell and Esther in the front hall and called out, "Magda's room."

I handed off the towels to Esther and stayed out of the room until the hot water was ready. When I took in the steaming basin, I handed it to Goldie and backed out of the room again.

There were enough people in the room already. Bell was questioning Goldie about untying Magda while Dr. Sampson was giving Esther directions on what to hand him. When he said he needed something to hold the towels in place, I stood in the hall and watched while Esther took the rope that had been tied around Magda's arms and showed it to the constable before handing it to the doctor.

"Constable, we need to move Mrs. Norris to my surgery so she'll be more comfortable while I stitch her up. Esther, can you come with us and act as nurse?"

"No," Peggy Norris said. "Someone go and get Rose Johnson. My daughter is staying with her. Bring her along to help." I noticed her voice sounded stronger. She was going to live.

And then I thought, she's going to live to attack me again.

With the doctor on one side and the constable on the other and Esther following, carrying the doctor's bag, they got Mrs. Norris to her feet and moved her slowly out of the house toward the doctor's surgery.

As he passed me, Bell said, "Call the inspector."

I nodded and followed them out into the long shadows of a late summer evening to hurry up the hill to the police house. Bell had left it unlocked so I walked in and sat at his desk to go through the drawers looking for an address book.

I should have realized it would be a file, with each page neatly typed. I found Inspector Grimsby's home telephone number in Oxford and called it.

He answered the call himself, as if he were expecting something to happen that night. I told him it was me calling, that the constable was with Mrs. Norris who was being sewn up by the doctor after trying to kill me—

"Don't be dramatic, Mrs. Redmond. Just tell me what happened."

"I am telling you what happened, inspector. She tied up our cook, Magda, and was waiting behind the door with a small kitchen knife for me to come in."

"They both got away from us," the inspector told me. "The son escaped across the border into Ireland, the Irish Free State, from Northern Ireland, and we lost the mother over there as well."

"Mrs. Norris came back here after unfinished business. Me," I exclaimed. "I think the constable wants you to come here tonight and take her prisoner."

"I was planning to come to Chipping Ford for a couple of days beginning tomorrow. My bag's all packed. I'll call Mr.

MacDonald, who is supposed to ride with me, and tell him to hurry if he wants to come along."

"Please hurry. Let me know when you get into town and arrest her so I can get some sleep tonight."

"Good to know someone will get some sleep tonight," Grimsby said drily before he hung up.

I closed the blackout curtains and left the constabulary house, walking toward the doctor's surgery. I wouldn't go in knowing the patient wanted me dead, but Magda came out and said, "Goldie is watching the children."

"Thank goodness for that. How is she doing?"

"Better than she should." Magda sounded fierce. "But she admitted to her daughter what she did, with Esther and me standing nearby."

"Did Dr. Sampson or Constable Bell hear her confess as well?"

"Both of them. Dr. Sampson got into a disagreement with her while he worked on her. He said she should have been glad Dr. Forrester diagnosed her son's asthma, because while it would not have saved him from clerical duties in some office, it would have saved him from combat."

It made sense to me, but I doubted it did to Peggy Norris. "What did she say to him?"

"London was as big a war zone as France was with all the bombing. She couldn't let him go to London. He might have been hurt. He might have been killed." Magda shook her head. "Some of us have lost entire families. She acts as if her son is worth more than all the rest of us combined."

"I'm sorry." I didn't know what else to say.

"I know, Livvy. Esther told me of some of your trips before the war. It was a good thing that you did." Magda squeezed my shoulder and then walked slowly back to the Old Vicarage.

I stood on the road for a while, hesitating between seeing if I could help in the surgery or checking on Stevie. My love for Stevie won out, even as I knew I could never kill to keep him out of combat. The army was his father's choice of occupation and I had to respect that, as well as the sanctity of human life.

Turning away from the surgery, I walked home.

* * *

Stevie, who was a perfect baby even on his off days, was wonderful and slept through until morning. I had him in his nappies and fed and dressed before Inspector Grimsby and Mr. MacDonald arrived in our front drawing room.

"Mrs. Peggy Norris has confessed to both murders and to attacking you and your cook. She won't say why, she won't discuss her son or his military deferment or where he is currently. She's being incredibly difficult," Grimsby told me.

"You've solved both murders. She's confessed. I would think you'd be happy," I said, sitting with Stevie on my lap.

"But she's refusing to testify against Dr. Embleton," Mr.

MacDonald said. "There's nothing to stop him from continuing to sell deferments or to keep the others who've bought deferments from using them."

"Perhaps if you came up to Oxford…" the inspector said.

Chapter Twenty-Six

"No!" I stood so abruptly that Stevie started to cry. I tried to soothe him as I calmed myself down. "It was one thing to find a killer in our little village. It's quite another to worry about military recruitment in another town. I have Stevie to think of, and I've left him with Esther and Goldie too much as it is."

"You're probably right," Mr. MacDonald said. "It's unfair of us to ask you to make an appointment at a doctor's surgery in Oxford and then learn what you can about the staff. Learn how to break into the doctor's surgery the same way you and Constable Bell did before."

"This is unfair and I won't do it." I tried not to be upset, but I was right. Their suggestion was unfair.

"Thank you for hearing us out, Mrs. Redmond." The two men rose from the couch and headed for the door.

"I wish you luck. You'll find a way to solve this case through another of his patients." I felt sure they would.

I let the two men out. When I did, Mr. MacDonald studied my face, but what he was looking for, I couldn't say. I looked back at him, wishing he would say what he was thinking.

But the moment passed and the two men left.

The day went quietly, interrupted by Sally the baker stopping Jane and me as we pushed our prams around the green to tell us Peggy Norris had been taken off in a police car. "I imagine she's on her way to Holloway Prison," the baker said with satisfaction. "They don't dare let her out or she'll escape again and attack someone here in Chipping Ford."

Definitely what I didn't want. I still had a bright scar down my arm from a scalpel on the night of the fire.

When she left, Jane asked, "Are you going to stay here, now that you've caught our killer?"

"Now I feel safe to," I assured her. "Now I know she's locked away in prison. Besides, I promised Lady Agatha I'd run the jam stall at the autumn festival."

Jane laughed the whole way down the green. When she stopped, I asked, "What's so funny?"

"That should be your reason to leave the village. Watch your back. There's nothing the ladies of this village will become homicidal about faster than their jam and whose is best."

"That's the type of homicidal person I feel safe around. The kind who might argue but wouldn't attack because they're relatively sane."

"Relatively," Jane agreed, still smiling widely.

Life went on. The Americans continued to invade Britain and were more or less welcomed. The Germans continued to fight the Russians. Adam managed to drop a clue that told me he was in Cairo, not Algeria, which was my other guess. His letters were as infrequent as ever, but I understood how difficult it was to get any word to me at all.

About two weeks later, I had just put Stevie down for his afternoon nap when there was a knock on the door. I went downstairs to answer and found Mr. MacDonald on the step. He came into the drawing room and asked how I was, looking warm on this hot, muggy day.

"Tea would be lovely," he agreed after we went through the pleasantries.

I went into the kitchen and found Magda had hot water and would bring us some tea. I went back out and said, "Tea will be ready in just a moment. Did you come to tell me that the trial has been scheduled?" No need to say which one.

"It had been, yes. But Peggy Norris killed herself in prison last night."

I dropped rather ungracefully onto a large chair, completely speechless.

"Everyone was after her to name Dr. Embleton as handing out deferments, and she always refused. I think she was afraid they would eventually deny any deferment the doctor handed out and her son would have to come in if he surfaced and retest with another doctor or be hunted down as a criminal."

I shook my head to clear the images crowding into my brain and then discovered Magda had poured our tea and Mr. MacDonald was thanking her.

"She killed herself." I was stunned.

"She knew we didn't have a case against the doctor if she didn't testify."

"Why not? There were other young men, other parents who must have paid the doctor," I said.

"She was the only one we had built a case against. The other parents aren't facing charges yet and therefore aren't as willing to divulge their sins."

"So, if the police keep at it, they should be able to find evidence to encourage other parents to talk," I suggested.

"That is our hope. That some other parent will testify rather than kill themselves," Mr. MacDonald said.

"That poor woman. Worried about her son to the last."

MacDonald took a sip of tea and said, "Very good, this."

I nodded. "Herbal. Magda works miracles with tea from weeds and flowers."

After a moment, MacDonald said, "Any parent would do practically anything for their child. I'm sure you would, Mrs. Redmond. Mrs. Norris just took it a step further."

"I guess her aunt and uncle will take in the Norris girl."

"That was written in a request that was found in her cell," MacDonald said.

"And the hunt will go on for Ben Norris?"

"I imagine they'll keep an eye out for him at the ports, but he's burrowed into Ireland and we'd never be able to find him if he stays there. In a neutral country? Maybe he'll resurface after the war." MacDonald set down his teacup and reached into his inner coat pocket.

"This has already been read by the police and the prison warden. I wish I didn't have to give it to you, but it is addressed to you, and you might find it enlightening."

He handed over one piece of writing paper folded once. I opened it and scanned the neat penmanship. It was signed,

I will haunt you forever, Peggy Norris

"I'll read it tonight. Maybe." Even as I said that, I knew she would haunt me if I didn't read this last message.

MacDonald rose and I followed him to the door. On the step, we shook hands and he said, "It was a pleasure working with you."

"And you. I hope your next posting is in as nice a place as Chipping Ford. We've enjoyed having you in the village," I told him with a smile.

"And I enjoyed living here. Goodbye, Mrs. Redmond."

"Goodbye, Mr. MacDonald." I watched him walk down the short path and out the gate toward the manor house where he had once worked.

When I shut the door, I put the letter on the mantelpiece and went to find Esther. She was in the kitchen with Magda and they were both going over cookery books.

"Mr. MacDonald come to say goodbye?" she asked me.

"Yes," I told her. "And to bring me a letter from Peggy Norris. She wrote it before she killed herself last night."

"That was never going to end well," Magda said in a firm tone. "She was too self-absorbed."

Esther looked shocked, but whether at my words or Magda's, I wasn't sure. "Who did she write it to?" she finally asked.

"She wrote it to me. I'd appreciate your presence when I read it tonight."

"She can't hurt you now, Livvy."

"I think she's going to, from beyond the grave."

After dinner that night, when the children were in bed and asleep, I went to the mantel and picked up the letter. Goldie and Magda took the couch, Esther claimed one chair by the cold fireplace, and I sat in the other.

Mrs. Redmond, I began to read out loud,

When you read this, I will no longer be available to be questioned, and so my son Ben and the other boys who went to Dr. Embleton will go free.

That is what is important, so I will answer your questions about the deaths of Mrs. Bryant, Mrs. Withins, and my mother. So far as I know, my mother died of an accident. I raised doubts because I was being blackmailed by Mrs. Bryant and I was setting the stage, so to speak, to make people wonder about her murder.

I knew Mrs. Bryant kept her back door unlocked so I entered that way. Unfortunately, the door can be seen from Mrs. Withins's kitchen. She saw me go in a while before blackout and a while later, just before blackout, she saw Constable Bell go in about her blackout curtains. Not closing the curtains was my first mistake.

Mrs. Withins found Mrs. Bryant's records listing how many she was blackmailing and how much and decided to take over the business. I went over to pay her one time and to scope out door locks and such things. I had no idea she was keeping Mrs. Bryant's records in Mrs. Bryant's house at that point and followed her through the back gardens.

Then you showed up and I had to flee before I could find the records. My second mistake was allowing you to find her records. After that, you were uncovering all her victims and proving them innocent of the killings, which meant you were bringing the crimes ever closer to me.

I knew you had broken into Dr. Sampson's surgery, but you hadn't made the connection between Ben's old medical records and his medical deferment. I didn't realize the smoke would blow into your window. Otherwise, I'd have just stolen his records. That was my third mistake.

What I don't understand is how a mother could hound another mother to her death when all she wanted was to keep her son safe. You have a son. Don't you want to keep him safe? If you are determined to be so righteous, then I hope your son is snatched away from you.

*You have ruined my life. Destroyed my happiness.
I will haunt you forever,*
Peggy Norris

I set down the letter and looked at the other three women I shared a house with. "What do you think?"

"Don't pay any attention to her. She killed two women. Didn't they deserve to have a life?" Esther said.

"Just burn it in the kitchen stove. It's worth no more than fuel for our tea," Magda said.

Goldie set down her knitting and said, "If all mothers thought that way, no one would be fighting Hitler. Why did she think she shouldn't have to worry when the rest of us are afraid every day?"

Goldie's sons had escaped Germany with her. The older was in the British army now and the younger would be old enough to serve next year.

Esther's James had left a highly lucrative job to use his skills to keep a section of the military functioning.

And Adam, still on crutches from wounds sustained in France, was now in Egypt either training troops or gathering intelligence. Or both.

"She's paid for her crimes. She deserves to be forgotten." The letter wasn't needed for any prosecutions. I rose and walked into the kitchen, burning her letter on the stove.

"And Mrs. Bryant's blackmail records?" Esther asked

when she followed me into the kitchen.

"The police have them. They'll never be used again. They may have already been destroyed, since they won't be needed for court cases."

"So, it's finished."

"Yes, thank goodness." Smiling, I followed Esther back to the drawing room, where we turned on the wireless to listen to what we hoped would be good news about the war.

And I prayed Adam would soon be safely home.

I hope you've enjoyed Deadly Village.

If you have, please be sure to read the rest of Olivia's adventures in The Deadly Series. And go to my website www.KateParkerbooks.com to sign up for my newsletter. When you do, you'll receive links to my free Deadly Series short stories you can download from BookFunnel onto the e-reader of choice.

If you want to let others know if you found Deadly Village to be a good read, leave a review at your favorite online retailer or tell your librarian. Reviews and recommendations are necessary for books to be discovered and to get good ratings. Thanks for your help on behalf of all good books.

Notes and Acknowledgements

The story at the beginning of Deadly Village with Olivia, Stevie, and the stove was taken from a story my grandmother told me about an event when my father was a baby. I hadn't thought of that tale in over fifty years until I started writing Deadly Village and realized how my grandmother's actions, transported to Olivia's father's home, would be the perfect opening. Fortunately, no one complained when my grandmother did this.

Much of the information I learned about the Women's Institute (WI) and the Mothers' Union I found in local newspapers of 1942 in the British Newspaper Archive, an online service of the British Library.

The children in the story are a blend of children I have observed over many years, including my own. Unfortunately, the idea of having a nanny never occurred to us at the time.

I have tried to demonstrate the effects of rationing and blackouts in the 1942 countryside in the lives of Livvy, Esther, and the villagers. In this age of instant communication, it is particularly hard to imagine waiting weeks for word from a loved one in a battle zone, but this would have been Olivia's reality.

I'd like to thank my first reader, my daughter Jennifer, my editors, Elizabeth Flynn and Les Floyd, my proofreader

Jennifer Brown, my formatter, Jennifer Johnson, and my cover artist, Lyndsey Lewellen. Their help has been invaluable in making this book as good as it can be. All mistakes, as always, are my own.

I thank you, my readers, for coming along with Olivia on this journey to the Cotswolds, murder, and new motherhood. I hope you've enjoyed it.

About the Author

Kate Parker grew up reading her mother's collection of mystery books by Christie, Sayers, and others. Now she can't write a story without someone being murdered, and everyday items are studied for their lethal potential. It had taken her years to convince her husband she hadn't poisoned dinner; that funny taste was because she couldn't cook. Her children have grown up to be surprisingly normal, but two of them are developing their own love of literary mayhem, so the term "normal" may have to be revised.

For the time being, Kate has brought her imagination to the perilous times before and during World War II in the Deadly Series. London society resembled today's lifestyle, but Victorian influences still abounded. Kate's sleuth is a young woman earning her living as a society reporter for a large daily newspaper while secretly working as a counterespionage agent for Britain's spymaster and finding danger as she tries to unmask Nazi spies while helping refugees escape oppression.

As much as she loves stately architecture and vintage clothing, Kate has also developed an appreciation of central heating and air conditioning. She's discovered life in Carolina requires her to wear shorts and T-shirts while drinking hot tea and it takes a great deal of imagination to picture cool, misty weather when it's 90 degrees out and sunny.

Follow Kate and her deadly examination of history at www.kateparkerbooks.com

And www.facebook.com/Author.Kate.Parker/

And www.bookbub.com/authors/kate-parker

Made in United States
North Haven, CT
15 September 2025